Praise for The High-R

"*The High-Rise Diver* is of
perfected capitalism. incing
world where every aspect of existence has been monetised.
In a taut, delicate narrative an implacable and disinterested
cruelty faces the human ache for tenderness, mercy,
contact and affection."
A.L. KENNEDY

"Straightforward and cool, the author's short, unadorned
sentences reveal how the promise of salvation through
greater efficiency, growth, and individual luck actually
represses, stifles, and destroys the very essence of life:
spontaneity, pain, dirt, emotion, poetry."
Frankfurter Allgemeine Zeitung

"A glistening novel about the blockade of welfare that is
closing in on the entire world."
CLEMENS SETZ, author of *Indigo*

"What makes Julia von Lucadou's novel so impressive is the
accuracy with which she describes this high-gloss, modern,
but by no means completely fictional world. Every detail is
so precise that, lurking beneath the flawlessness of the text,
the central theme of perfidious self-optimization seems to
always be present."
Süddeutsche Zeitung

"Julia von Lucadou's science fiction cuts close. Against the
backdrop of the gleaming images used to portray this
Orwellian-style city-state, the tragic moments of direct
human encounters take on a dimension of clever criticism."
Spiegel Online

"The author's precision in depicting the process of decay, later marked by delusional episodes, is the explosive force behind this text. It meticulously states the consequences of a society governed by totalitarian control and optimization. Welcome to neo-liberalism 4.0!"
Berliner Zeitung

"In literary and discursive terms, the most exciting debut of the autumn season."
Kulturnews

"With clear analysis and precision, Julia von Lucadou describes the merciless surveillance of the world of big data."
Inforadio

"*The High-Rise Diver* is a highly intelligent, prescient, and entertaining novel about our brave new world of voluntary surveillance. An outstanding debut!"
WDR

The High-Rise Diver

Published in the USA in 2021 by World Editions LLC, New York
Published in the UK in 2021 by World Editions Ltd., London

World Editions
New York / London / Amsterdam

Printed by Lake Book, USA

Library of Congress Cataloging in Publication Data is available

ISBN 978-1-64286-076-4

First published as *Die Hochhausspringerin* in 2018 by Hanser Berlin im
Carl Hanser Verlag GmbH & Co. KG, München

This book was published with the support of the Swiss Arts Council
Pro Helvetia

swiss arts council
prohelvetia

Twitter: @WorldEdBooks
Facebook: @WorldEditionsInternationalPublishing
Instagram: @WorldEdBooks
www.worldeditions.org

Book Club Discussion Guides are available on our website.

Julia von Lucadou

The High-Rise Diver

Translated from the German
by Sharmila Cohen

WORLD EDITIONS
New York, London, Amsterdam

For Waiteata

The woman is perfected.
Her dead
Body wears the smile of accomplishment,
The illusion of a Greek necessity
Flows in the scrolls of her toga,
Her bare
Feet seem to be saying:
We have come so far, it is over.

  "Edge"
   Sylvia Plath

Imagine the world.

Imagine the globe floating in space.

From your vantage point, the world is round and smooth. Enjoy its uniformity; imagine that it exists only for you. Close your eyes for a moment, take a deep breath in and out. After a few seconds, open your eyes again and consider the earth anew.

Now zoom in a little closer. You can make out irregularities in the evenness of the earth's surface, elevations and depressions. They form a soft, undulating relief. The shifts from red to blue to brown create a mottled pattern.

As you get closer, a silver fleck stands out against this earth-colored display. What you see here, from afar but steadily approaching, is a city. It glistens because it is made of glass and steel, you can see that now. The city lies beneath you like a secret waiting to be revealed. So zoom in at ease, don't be shy, you're allowed to look.

You find it reassuring to see that the city also maintains a sort of uniformity; the buildings conform to an architectural style and are arranged geometrically in rectangular and star formations. Side by side, the almost delicate-looking skyscrapers are indistinguishable as they reach up into the atmosphere.

The city is now unfolding beneath you, an infinite sea. And yet it has an end, an edge, back there, where clouds of dust and exhaust fumes rise into the sky. Must it be this way, you think, must the beautiful city be tainted by the sight of filth? Why must it end anywhere at all? But can you imagine the sea without the beach or the cliff or the pier? No, without the peripheries, without its repulsive exterior, the city, now shimmering in the orange afternoon light, would only be half as beautiful.

Concentrate on the center of the city. One of the skyscrapers rises above the others by several dozen floors.

There's a color deviation around the building. At first it looks like an image error, but then, as you zoom in, it turns out to be matter, moving, alive. Between the structures you can see a swarming cluster, densely packed heads, a crowd of people. It vibrates, the heads move, and then you see what the crowd is waiting for down there: There's a glittering object on the roof of that imposing tower.

In the close-up, you realize it's a woman in a silvery suit. The flysuit™ conforms to the contours of her well-toned physique, making her every curve and shape visible, so that she appears almost naked.

Consider the woman's face. What a face, you think, so symmetrical, as if someone had just created half and then mirrored it. It's a young face, the woman is maybe twenty years old, you suppose, at the height of her beauty, her body taut, her eyes wide open. Look closely at those eyes, you will not find a single blemish, no redness, no clouding of the irises or unequal pupil dilation. Instead, sharp focus, concentration. What you see is a professional athlete at work. Every one of this woman's muscles is under control. If you asked her to describe the feeling in her right big toe, she could do so with great precision.

At this very moment, a jolt passes through her body; she moves to the edge of the roof. It's time. Maybe you would like to pull away a little, out of the close-up, and open up your view to what lies below. The corridor between the buildings is a one-thousand-meter drop, precisely one thousand meters of altitude, as defined by the guidelines of the Global Committee for High-Rise Diving™.

The audience holds its breath as the woman steps to the outermost edge of the flat roof. She has a supernatural shimmer in her flysuit™. The people on the ground and in the viewing boxes on the opposite building—all the way up to the skybox™—reach their arms up towards her.

What you're experiencing is a physical manifestation of euphoria. It pulsates between the buildings. Close your eyes. Let it infect you. Feel what's happening inside you. Feel it down to your fingertips, feel your heart throbbing as the feeling spreads throughout your body.

When you open your eyes, the woman is diving head-first from the skyscraper roof.

At first you're scared. Your body tenses up as if it were falling beside her.

But then you see the diver as a bird in flight. You feel her absolute certainty that she will be able to withstand the fall.

You follow the falling body, stay close to it. You see how it rotates around itself with perfect precision, first horizontally, then vertically, twisting into a ball and then stretching out again within fractions of a second. In the next moment, you see the ground. It fills your field of vision, you hold your breath. She is plummeting towards it, threatening to crash. The hot sun-drenched asphalt is already palpable when her body suddenly shoots up, lifted by the flysuit's™ flight mode, triggered at the last possible moment, fractions of a second before impact.

You can hear the air being released from the open mouths of the audience, a collective exhale.

The crowd applauds, the diver shoots like an arrow into the sky. In flight, she smiles into the cameras, a weightless figure.

Imagine how this woman feels, falling into the depths with unwavering certainty, knowing you will take flight again. Without any fear of impact, of obliteration.

You enjoy defying gravity; death can no longer harm you. What a feeling, weightlessness. What a sublime feeling.

Now back away again, zoom out slowly, carefully, without shaking, so that the movement remains pleasant to the eye. Imagine that the body between the buildings rises and falls again and again, even when you can no longer recognize it as a body, when it's just a spot in motion, then a point, a possible pixel error, and then nothing at all. You zoom out and see the globe floating in space again, uniform and calm.

Imagine the body in its eternity, immortal, its continuous rising and falling, like breathing, like a pulse. Savor this thought, take refuge in it, draw confidence from it. Now, in this moment, as you slowly withdraw from the world, there is no death, only life.

1

This is how I see Riva today: playing with a plastic top like a child. Legs spread, upper body hunched forward. I can hear the sound of the top filling her apartment, the monotonous humming. Then, the top falls to the side. Her hand reaches for it. I see the hand, hear spinning, humming, silence, spinning, humming, silence, in an endless loop.

I wonder whether this game can be described as a compulsive act. And where she got a hold of the toy. Maybe it's going through a revival on some lifestyle blog, a trend that will be forgotten in a few months' time.

I see Riva's long, white, outstretched legs. Her summer dress clings to her body, her chest glistens with sweat. *Refusal to turn on the air conditioning*, I make a note and in the comment column: *Self-castigation / indication of feelings of guilt?*

There's too much light, the picture is overexposed. The neighboring buildings reflect the sun in through the wide windows. I adjust the monitor's brightness.

The sound of the top drones in my ears. I feel slight nausea and the onset of a cluster headache around my right eye. I concentrate on my breathing to prevent an attack, in and out.

The image on the monitor blurs before my eyes. Ice cubes clatter against the side of my water glass. I hold it to my forehead and let the condensation run down my nose.

The weather forecast for the next three days: heat, no rain, air quality index poor, fine dust pollution high.

Condensation drips down into my cleavage. I put the glass down to refill the ice and start the game over again: forehead, nose, mouth, chest.

Suddenly, a piercing notification beep. I look for the tablet on my desk. It's blinking silently. The sound is not my sound; it's coming from the monitor speakers, slightly distorted. I pivot the camera away from Riva and around the room until I spot the tablet on her coffee table.

Riva doesn't respond.

After twenty seconds, she begins to imitate the sound, beeping like a machine.

My temple throbs, I turn down the volume.

Your stress hormone levels are too high, Masters said. You need to take better care of yourself. Meditation, relaxation exercises. Conscious breathing. Avoid noise.

On the monitor a door opens. Aston appears in the door-frame. He runs to the tablet and taps on the screen. The beeping stops. My neck muscles relax.

—For fuck's sake, can't you turn it off yourself!

I note Riva's evasive demeanor, the reflexive way she draws her legs in towards her body. *Defensive posture*, I write, and in the research column: *Indication of domestic violence?* So far, the data analysis has shown no evidence of it.

Aston turns on the air conditioning. At the window, he lifts his camera to his face and looks down at the city through the lens. I have not seen him in the apartment without a camera since this project began. He wears it on a strap around his neck so that it protrudes like a tumor at stomach level.

Aston seems most vulnerable, most himself when taking a photo. The moment is so intimate that I almost feel uncomfortable watching it. His half-open mouth tenses behind the camera as he focuses; the corners of his lips sinking back down as they relax after the shutter release.

In the overhead shot, the living room appears to fray around the edges, with the space divided into segments like individual rays of light. Aston has installed partition walls with digital picture frames perpendicular to the wall in order to maximize the space. The continuously alternating images are like advertising loops on a taxi screen. There is something narcissistic about the way he turns their precious shared living space into his own personal gallery. Every night he uploads new photographs before going to bed. The pictures from the past few weeks: all the same high-rise-complex perspective, a bird's-eye view of ant-sized heads and toy-sized vehicles in various formations. In my first daily report, I put forward the hypothesis that this is an empathic exercise. The attempt to put himself in his partner's position, a partner whose only remaining connection to the outside world is the view from the window.

With its own partition wall in the middle, Aston's magnum opus *Dancer_of_the_Sky*™ is on four thirty-two-inch digiframes on a ten-minute loop. It's the photo series that made him an overnight success four years ago. Images of Riva diving, Riva in the air, her elongated form between the rows of buildings, her body precisely aligned, her hands stretched out above her head like a ballet dancer. Her body silver and sparkling in the flysuit™. Using an exposure technique, Aston manipulated the light reflecting from the skyscraper walls, burning out the background around her. A sacred superhero swooping down from the heavens.

The constant clicking of Aston's shutter blends with the sound of Riva repeatedly spinning her top. The rhythmically contoured soundscapes are almost melodic. An unintentional ensemble.

I make note of the effect in another column of the log. As the amount of data grows, so does the need for marking systems, a means of organization that facilitates analysis. Only when enough information has been made available does the noteworthy become visible, subtle breaks and contradictions, the underlying structures, the inner drives.

It's a little like factory work, this first step, taking notes on the everyday. My observations repeat themselves as regularly as Aston's photographs in their frames. Riva on the floor, Riva with the top, Riva sweating in the sun. Aston coming out of the studio and adjusting the temperature.

—You know, it was another summons, he says now, holding up the tablet.

I see from my log that he said the same sentence two days ago with the same wording. I wonder which sentences I repeat daily without noticing.

Aston has put the tablet aside and is holding his camera to his chest. He mostly only uses the other cameras as backup. This is a vintage model, produced about twenty years ago. Aston's financial transactions indicate that he bought it three months ago from the second largest online reseller.

—You pay a fine every time you don't respond. You'll be paying until there's nothing left. And then we'll keep paying somehow.

Riva acts like she doesn't hear him. She reaches for the top, forcing Aston to talk over the sound.

—Aren't you afraid that your muscles will degenerate? At some point you won't be able to stand up anymore. It happens faster than you think.

Riva shrugs and reaches for the top, stops it in motion, and spins it again. I'm also concerned about her body's rapid deterioration, the progressive muscular atrophy and weight loss. Ever since she broke her contract, Riva has refused to undergo her compulsory examinations and no longer wears her activity tracker. There is no way to determine her fitness data with certainty, but it's obvious that she's getting worse every day.

—Your body needs vitamin D, Aston says in a slightly different tone, more caring, more urgent. More natural light.

I am impressed by his commitment, the patience with which he dedicates himself to her every day, trying to get closer to her.

—That's in the nutritional water, Riva says with her face turned away.

I add one to the daily count of her spoken sentences. So far there has been no fundamental improvement in her willingness to communicate.

Aston has left his post at the window without me noticing. He stops about a meter away from Riva and then slowly walks around her. He looks at her from all sides, tilts his head, squats. Then he starts taking pictures of her.

—I have an idea for a new project, he says.

Riva's hand reaches for the top. It slips out of her fingers too soon and only spins for a few seconds.

I observe a change of mood in Aston's facial features: impatience, open frustration.

—Just because you quit your career doesn't mean I have to lose my job, he says. You're messing with my life, too.

There's a shrill alarm sound outside, police sirens. I don't know if it's coming from the speaker or through my office window.

The apartment is suddenly quiet; Riva has put down the top. She looks out the window, her eyes don't appear to be focused on anything in particular.

I hear Aston breathing quickly and loudly, three, four times. There are these moments when he briefly loses control. His body is possessed by anger, impatience. His facial muscles are strained, his body tense.

Then he calms down, relaxes his shoulders, reaches out to touch Riva. He runs his index finger down her slightly curved back, tracing her spine.

—You're too thin. I can see your bones.

Riva doesn't move.

In my comment column I note: *Passive behavior, Karnovsky submits to the role of object.*

—Come on, Riva.

Aston grabs her shoulder and shakes it gently, but her unresponsiveness seems to discourage him, he doesn't persist long.

He turns away and goes back to the window, reaches for the camera on his stomach. The usual click echoes through the room, both are back in their positions, appearing more like silhouettes than people against the light.

I lean back and watch them, my subject and her partner in the rectangular frame of the live monitor. Next to it, on my work monitor, a chat window is blinking; on the desk, also blinking, the tablet; under the table, a discarded flatscreen, ready to be picked up.

I click through the video files in the data archive. The analyst has uploaded four recordings of Riva and Aston's apartment from the time before Riva's breach of contract. They come from private providers. Four files from the last four years, taken on the first of August each year when the security systems were tested in all of the apartments in the building.

I open the most recent file on the work monitor and then I adjust the camera position on the live monitor so that both screens show the same detail. A wide shot of the apartment from above. With the two screens side by side, it's almost impossible to tell the images apart— there are just a few more of Aston's photo walls now.

For the first several hours, the archive video shows the empty apartment. Only the lighting changes when watched in time-lapse mode. The security camera's automatic aperture control adjusts the brightness. Wandering shadows from the furniture on the smooth designer floor.

Around 7 p.m., Riva enters the apartment in her training clothes. She puts down her sports bag, goes to the kitchen, and turns on the water. She tests the water temperature with her index finger, washes her face, and strips down to her underwear.

For a moment, she just stands in the room, lost in thought, forgetting her surroundings. Then she goes to the fridge to get a drink.

Liger™, a sports drink. One of her sponsors.

She sits at the window, looking down from the sixty-fourth floor. Her body is perfect in every respect, her spine straight, her skin glowing and smooth. She opens her ponytail and her hair cascades over her shoulders, shining in the evening light. The security video is almost indistinguishable from an advertising clip. Everything is perfect: lighting, positioning, and model.

Riva sits at the window in her light gray athletic undergarments, takes a sip from the bottle, looks down. She's probably going over the day's training sessions in her mind, remembering the failed and successful maneuvers, the new jumps. The video ends when Aston enters through the door that connects his studio to the living room. He sees his partner, picks up his camera, and shoots. Riva, hearing the click of the device, looks over her shoulder at him and smiles. I have unsuccessfully tried to find the photo in Aston's archives. I write a note to my assistant to look for the photo again and attach a screenshot of the video.

I would have liked to observe Riva back then. To see her train, the movement of her muscles under her taut skin, the strength and control of a highly conditioned body.

I attended my first high-rise diving™ show when I was six years old. I remember how it felt, getting off the bus two-by-two, my whole body trembling and tense with excitement.

It was my first trip with the talent scout program. A look into the future, if we were lucky. A motivation trip™ meant to inspire us to greatness. What do you want to become? A high-rise diver. To risk falling, so you can soar, as our career trainers said. The closer you get to death, the more alive you become. We had cheap tickets. Not a box, just standing room on the ground. At least it wasn't far from the fall spot™, a closed-off area on the ground that the divers were supposed to aim for, to get as close to it as possible. At the time I had still not seen the videos of accidents, of technical failures. Blood-sprayed spectators, barriers coming out of the ground, people in waterproof orange suits.

Back then, there was only anticipation. I was wedged between adults who towered over me. The smell of sweat, a herd smell that was foreign to me and unexpected.

High above us, the diving platform couldn't be seen from the ground. At least I managed to peer through a space between two men and see part of a monitor showing the event from different camera angles.

I felt the sound waves in my body. The audience cheering when the first diver appeared on the platform. We all stretched our arms up into the air as far as we could.

Then, the shock when the diver jumped, plummeting at an unfathomable speed.

The falling body, as if heading straight for me. The suit's shimmer, the diver's outstretched fingers, my relief as she shot back up, just inches above the ground.

Our joint sigh of relief and then her ascent, accompanied by thunderous applause.

If I want to make it home before the night shift starts for my second job, I should leave now. Forty-five minutes to drive home, seventy-five minutes for dinner and mindfulness exercises.

The evening light is a different color on the monitor than in my office. This may be due to the location. Riva and Aston's apartment is dozens of floors higher than here, the difference in natural light is measurable.

My right hand rubs my temple. The gesture has taken on a life of its own, has almost become a sort of tick. The headache is a constant, it swells and subsides like the tides. A consequence of stress, says Masters. Meditation, relaxation exercises. Conscious breathing. Avoid noise.

A full-blown headache attack on the way home would be hard to bear. I would have to stop driving and lie down on the back seat. Close my eyes. Wait until it passes.

Powerless against this force of nature.

Maybe I should stay a few more minutes. Massage my neck. Lower my heart rate, which is currently displayed at eighty-three on the activity tracker. Take a deep breath. Avoid noise.

Riva has started spinning the top again. I turn the monitor volume to zero. When the monotonous scraping noise is muted, I feel a wave of relaxation. In the background, only the soft hum of my devices.

A green check mark in the chat window indicates that my assistant is still logged in. I send him a message.

Are you still there?

Yes.

You can sign off now.

On my securecloud™ file list, I can see Masters accessing my document. If he's still in the office, it might be a good idea to stay a bit longer, show commitment. Then again, he rarely says goodbye, so he could have left several hours ago and logged into the system from home. Maybe I can nonchalantly walk past his office. But it's the last door in the hall, my intentions would be obvious right away.

I could also just start my night shift here, and why not, I get the fewest client calls at shift start anyway. I can postpone dinner and meditation a little, and interrupt them later for a consultation if necessary.

The overtime will increase my employee ranking. I'm in the upper third of my division. Masters gave my first five reports high ratings. Probably to give me a boost as a beginner. It worked. When I get tired, looking at the standings and seeing my upward curve motivates me more than my nootropics.

When I glance back at the live monitor, Aston and Riva are still in the same positions. Aston at the window with his camera, Riva on the floor. If it weren't for the top spinning on the ground, you'd think the picture was frozen.

Archive No.: M14_b
File Type: M-Message™
Sender: @DomWuAcademy
Recipient: @PsySolutions_ID5215d

Ms. Yoshida,
As discussed, here is my report on the aforementioned conversation with Riva, which took place ten days before her breach of contract. I tried to describe Riva's statements and my observations with as much precision and detail as possible. I can't guarantee that all of the information provided, insofar as it concerns my personal perception of the situation, is 100% accurate. Unfortunately, the conversation was not recorded on video, but only as an audio note. If you have any questions, please do not hesitate to contact me. We hope you'll be able to revive Riva as soon as possible. As I told you at the steering committee meeting, I am not merely concerned about the great financial damage and loss of face incurred by my company and our sponsors, but primarily about Riva's health.
    Yours sincerely, Dom Wu

Attachment: Report_Wu_Karnovsky_I.arc
The conversation took place on July 18th at 5:30 p.m. and lasted almost twenty minutes. I asked Riva into my office to discuss her current scores. She had shown no progress in the previous weeks—no major deficits either—but there was a distinct change in her disposition, that is, her social

behavior and mood. Although she showed up at all of her training sessions, she seemed unmotivated to me, which didn't correspond with her usual personality. From the start of her career, Riva was a very ambitious, energetic person. She had good social interactions with her teammates and, in addition to training, she was also interested in art and literature. She seemed balanced, neither overly excitable in the sense of being manic nor tending towards sadness. When she lost tournaments or did poorly in training, she quickly overcame her initial frustration and turned it into a thirst for action.

I spoke to Riva directly about her changed behavior. She reacted evasively, trying to change the topic to the results. I asked her if something had happened. She denied it, but avoided direct eye contact.

I reproduce our conversation here to the extent that the audio recording allows:
—You can trust me. (Me)
—I know. I trust you. (Riva)
—If something's bothering you, we have to talk about it. It hurts your performance if you don't deal with personal problems properly.
—I know.
—Are you unwell?
—I just have a headache. I don't feel so good.
—Have you seen a doctor?
—It's not that bad.
Riva's last mandatory examination had been four days earlier. Her vital score index™ was as high as always. Riva has rarely had to struggle with injuries or other health problems. She is physically very healthy.
—I'm worried about you. (Me)
—You don't have to be. (Riva)

At about this point in the conversation, Riva took my hand and squeezed it. As already stated on the log, we were always very close. Riva has often confided in me on private matters. Through many years of working together professionally, we have built up a familial closeness that includes sporadic hugs and other similar forms of physical contact. This is undoubtedly also the reason why there have been occasional false reports in the media about us having an affair. I feel connected to her in an almost paternal way. That is, in the sense of an old-fashioned, romanticized ideal of biopaternity, but I can't think of a better comparison. I have been beside Riva since she was nine years old and, although I don't value the other girls any less, she has always been somehow special to me. Of course, this may also have something to do with her outstanding performance.

I squeezed her hand and asked her again what was wrong. I could feel that her initial reluctance had eased somewhat. She gave me a longer answer:

—You know the feeling when your credit level rises and you get higher living-space privileges? You move in to your new apartment, look at the new surroundings, maybe go to the roof garden. You see it all for the first time and it inspires you, your wide windows, your view from above the city, the clean streets, the beautifully trimmed boxwoods in the roof garden, the small platform with the bench, and so on. Then you see it every day, three times a week you sit on that bench and the picture loses a little bit of color each time, until at some point everything—the window, the street, the park—it just makes you sick, you can't look at it anymore.

—It's perfectly normal for things to get boring. Maybe you should move again.

—That's not the point! I don't just mean the apartment, I mean my whole life. The diving, Aston, everything.

—But now you're exaggerating. You're in a bad mood. Maybe you should take a day off, do something nice, let Aston take you somewhere special. Or I can book you a happiness training™ session. Something like that.

—You don't get what I mean.

—Of course I get it, Riva. You've been diving for fifteen years, you're worried. You're bored. Maybe you're thinking about what you should do when your body stops cooperating at some point. But you're in great shape. You're at the top of all the leaderboards. The younger competitors can't touch you. You have a realistic chance of winning the World Championships.

—What difference does it make if I win the World Championships or not?

I tried to make her feel better, but Riva contradicted everything I said. She seemed unmovable, bitter. I assumed it was just a phase, so I didn't press her too hard. In retrospect, I realize that I probably should have been more persistent and just ordered her to go to happiness training™.

Riva ended the conversation. She said she had a headache and wanted to lie down. We briefly went over the training schedule for the next day and she seemed to rally her spirits a bit.

I took her hand again; she quickly pulled away, but smiled at me.

—Everything's gonna be okay.™ (Me)

—You haven't said that to me in a long time. (Riva, still smiling)

—You haven't needed it in a long time.

—Don't worry, Dom.

With that, she left my office.

I left the conversation with a good feeling, since her smile seemed authentic to me, as if something had been resolved, something fundamental inside her.

2

My tablet rings and wakes me up at 2:33 a.m. Ever since I started regularly working the night shift, I only need a few seconds to shake the heaviness of sleep from my body when I get up. Like a bird that sleeps with only one half of its brain.

I'm still at the office. I must have nodded off while looking at the archive documents. My neck hurts from the awkward sleeping position. I had my head on the desk, now my right cheek has an imprint from the edge of my tablet.

—How can I help you?

Although the caller is using her employer's internal Call-a-Coach™ hotline, the system doesn't recognize her identification number or her language profile. I don't understand her name, her voice is distorted and interrupted by sobs.

—Where are you calling from?

—From home, I'm home.

—From your tablet? Your number is not registered.

—It's new. It's a new device.

—Okay, I see.

—Is that a problem?

—No. Of course not. What happened?

She keeps sniffling. The sound makes my body tense up. One by one, each muscle stiffens, intensifying my neck pain. I can't block out the image of the caller's mucus being sucked back continuously.

—Try to take deep breaths. In. Out. In. Out. You see.

—What should I do now? she asks in a soft, strained voice. What am I supposed to do now?

—May I ask you to describe the situation to me from the beginning? Unfortunately, I didn't catch your name.

—Talin, she says in an unexpectedly official tone. Omega Talin. My search yields fifteen results on her employer's intranet employee list with that last name, but none with the first.

—Ms. Talin, which department do you work in?

—Kash Talin, she says with a slowly diminishing voice, as if someone were turning down the volume. I'm Kash Talin's partner, he's head of media relations for app content.

—What happened exactly?

She breathes, swallows, sniffs back the mucus again.

—He's cheating on me. He has someone else. He didn't come home. I read his messages. What am I supposed to do now? If he leaves me, I'll have to go back to the peripheries. We have a credit union. I lost my job three weeks ago. My life is over.

On the online feedback form I estimate the acute suicide risk at forty percent, but then correct it down to thirty. Under reason for call I enter: *partner/affair*, under next actions: *inform head of media relations*.

I type a short message to Kash Talin, subject: *Urgent!*

—Are you sure the messages are real? Ms. Talin? Omega?

Your wife suspects an affair. Call me. I press send.

Ms. Talin breathes out, in, out. I imagine her chest rising and falling beneath her thin nightgown. Damp with cold sweat from the physical strain of panic.

—I don't know. They're on his private account … He hasn't come home.

The acknowledgement of receipt comes immediately. I select the automatic response: *still on the phone with her*, and add: *I'll let you know when the line is free.*

—Ms. Talin, here's what we're going to do: together, we'll go through a relaxation exercise, a visualization, a short inner journey. This will give your mind and body a little rest in order to help you think clearly again. Okay?

—Okay.

Her voice is still quieter than normal.

—We're going to get through this.

—Okay.

—We're going to sort it all out.

After I hang up with her, I talk to Kash Talin briefly.

—End your affair, I say. You know what the end of a primary relationship does to productivity. Consider how much you want to stay in your relationship, assign it a percentage. If it's over fifty percent, do something about it.

I send him links to partner coaching sessions and online guides for long-term relationships.

My ranking is immediately updated in the Call-a-Coach™ app on my tablet. I received the highest score for both the customer rating and the client rating on the tracking tool. It'll only take a few more coaching sessions before I get promoted to master coach in my profile. I spend the rest of the night in a free bunk in the room-of-rest™ because it's not worth going home at this point.

3

—I don't get you, Aston says.

Lately, whenever he talks to Riva, he leaves gaps where the answers would go. As if they could be added later.

—You have everything, Aston says. We're doing fine. Why do you just want to throw it away?

He lets his eyes wander across the designer furniture. Styled by a well-known interior designer, the sprawling living room has been featured several times on architecture blogs. In one of the most sought-after districts, reserved for VIPs and top earners. Riva and Aston live only three floors below the penthouse. Their view of the city is breathtaking. The natural light is particularly intense today. I constantly have to adjust the screen brightness whenever I change the camera view. I imagine the daylight slowly diminishing with each floor beneath them and then only artificial light remaining on the lowest level.

—You earned it all, Aston says. You worked so hard.

Riva is silent. She is sitting on the floor again, but closer to the window today, so she can look out. The top is nowhere to be seen. You can't tell whether she's actually looking at something outside or if she's lost in her own thoughts.

—What if I don't want to work hard, she says at some point.

I highlight the sentence bright yellow.

—Then what do you want?

Riva is silent. I set the daily count of her spoken sentences to one.

According to the relationship profile created by the data analyst, Aston and Riva met almost five years ago at a morning event, an exhibition opening featuring works by a photographer who had just published an editorial on Riva. One of Aston's former classmates, more successful and well known than he was at the time.

There are many photos of their first meeting, but relatively few papavids™. After the brand Rivaston™ was established, the little existing video footage was posted and reposted in the lifestyle media and on Riva's brand apps. New versions continuously appeared, recut and with new commentary.

Aston must have recognized her from a distance, Riva Karnovsky, the high-rise diver. The press photographs from the event are staged to show her as the epitome of youth. Lively and impetuous, like a teenager in an overpriced designer dress. Her cheeks rosy, probably from alcohol, which her nutritional profile allows only for special occasions.

According to the editor of a society blog, Riva's face was beaming when she told them about her first conversation with Aston a few days later.

Aston reached out to shake with one hand, while offering me a glass of champagne with the other. I had no idea who he was. His smile blew me away. I come to your performances as often as I can, he said, you're an absolutely enchanting dancer. I said: Diver, you mean. No, dancer, he said—the way you move in the air, you dance, we forget that you're hundreds of feet above the ground. When I watch you, I hear music in my head. And I said: Maybe you should talk to a doctor about that?

Most of the photos from the evening already portray the two as a couple. Riva in the center, Aston at the edge of the picture, but present, broad-shouldered. In some pictures you can see the excitement on his face. He must have felt electrified by the public attention he had previously been denied.

Media analysts initially speculated that they had known each other for weeks, if not months before that. They seemed to have a sense of familiarity in their movements, they were always turned slightly towards each other. Riva took his hand as she directed the vjs, showed the cameras her distinctive profile, changed poses, gave witty statements.

From the start of her career, Riva was naturally talented at dealing with the media. She managed to put her own spin on the standard answers from the academy's interview guide, so that they never sounded rehearsed or boring. After competitions, she took time for fans and the press. Smiled away her exhaustion. Answered the same questions over and over again with an air of authentic enthusiasm. Even before her first international victories, her advertising contracts were valued above the industry average.

In the first year of their relationship, Aston, the handsome underdog, was primarily seen as Riva's accessory, a boy toy in a series of boy toys. He only earned his status as an autonomous individual with the publication of his photo series *Dancer_of_the_Sky™*.

—What can I do, Riva? What do you want from me?

In the current camera perspective, a medium shot with Aston in the foreground, he seems taller than he actually is. Almost oversized compared to Riva, who is sitting on the floor in the background, hunched forward.

His arms hang down on both sides of his upper body like foreign objects. As if he wouldn't know what to do with them if they weren't operating the camera around his neck.

—Nothing, Riva says, I don't want anything from you at all, Aston.

Her tone reminds me of the educators at my childcare institute when they had to answer our questions.

The most popular internet conspiracy theory about Riva's resignation is that it has to do with relationship drama, that Riva left Aston for someone else and that he's now forcing her to stay with him against her will. A well-known gossip blog regularly posts drone videos of them in their apartment, alleging violent situations. Analysis has shown that the images are current, but were manipulated after the fact. Fans post comments daily on Riva's official website, encouraging her to be brave and urging the police to arrest Aston. Building security has been reporting break-in attempts by fans trying to "free" Riva.

During the case-history briefing, Dom Wu pointed out that there had been multiple rumors over the past year about one of them having an affair. The data analyst tagged and examined all blog and news entries on the topic. His report notes that no useful photo or video material exists to confirm the rumors. The posts are all complete hearsay or misinterpreted recordings of harmless public appearances when Aston and Riva were in the company of colleagues or fans.

However, we can't entirely rule out the possibility, writes the analyst, *that the* PR *department at the academy has had some incriminating material removed. Still, there are no direct indications of this. To date, Dom Wu and his staff have been cooperative and accommodating in every respect.*

Various sources accuse Wu of having an affair with Riva Karnovsky, as well as other students at the academy. Evidence of the court proceedings and out-of-court settlements cited in the articles could not be found in any of the legal databases.

The data analyst added the metatags *affair* and *Dom Wu* to the relevant posts. They include photos and papavids™ of the two of them at training. Instances when Wu touches Riva, cut and edited in such a way that the physical contact could be interpreted sexually.

—You can dissolve the credit union for all I care, Riva says.

I set the daily count of her spoken sentences to three. *Slight improvement in willingness to communicate*, I write in the comment column.

Aston doesn't react immediately. He raises his shoulders. He turns away from Riva and goes to one of the photo walls. He touches one of the frames with his right hand. The picture is from the *Dancer_of_the_Sky*™ series. Riva from behind, on the diving platform, slightly blurred. Most of the image is taken up by the roof, which stretches out like a runway in front of her. A little generic. The body in the flysuit™ could just as easily be another jumper.

—You were so happy, Aston says without turning around. When I took the photos. Do you remember? You once told me you were the happiest person I'd ever meet.

I zoom in on Riva's face to get a better look at her reaction. Masters advised me to use facial-interpretation software for my analysis, but moments like these are what I love most about my work. Moments of sudden understanding, like now, when Riva drops her mask of apathetic indifference and her face tells a story. The corners of her mouth shift by fractions of an inch, turn up, a barely perceptible smile. Nostalgic. Remembering better times. Then her eyes widen, she looks up, her jaw tenses, she clenches her teeth together. Her gaze turns to her partner, who still has his back to her. Lips pressed firmly together, a slight retraction of the lower lip.

With such high resolution, the image on the monitor sometimes appears clearer than reality. More precise.

Riva turns away again, looks down at her hands in her lap. Her facial expression returns to its former indifference, resignation. The facial muscles relax except for the eyebrows, which pull slightly together.

—That's true, she says. That's what I said back then.

Aston looks over at her, letting go of the picture frame. I select the camera closest to him, so that I can look over his shoulder. See what he sees. Riva on the floor in her summer dress, her hands in her lap, her head lowered. Almost a cliché. The fragile little girl. The damsel in distress.

Aston walks into the shot towards her. He sits next to her. He puts his arm around her back and lets his head drop onto her shoulder.

She withdraws. Almost in slow motion. Gradually moving away from him, so that he has to reposition himself upright in order to avoid toppling over.

No matter what type of physical closeness Aston attempts, Riva's reaction is always the same: to evade or squirm away. Never a recoil, which might be interpreted as fear or disgust. Instead, a neutral, slow retreat, like a snail winding its way into its shell, a fraction of an inch at a time.

In the five and a half days since the live analysis began, there has only been one clearly sexual advance. At 10:17 p.m. on the second day of observation, Riva went into the bedroom. Aston followed her. I watched in night vision mode as Aston lay behind Riva and wrapped his arms around her. She slowly moved away from him and towards the wall, he followed. There was no talking. You could only hear the blanket rustling, suggesting more movement than was visible. I switched to the camera in the wall at bed level. It showed Riva from the front, her frozen stare, Aston's face behind her, his eyes closed. He kissed her neck. She remained in her position. There was no more space in front of her to escape to. He pushed up her nightgown. She continued staring at the wall. Aston pressed closer to her. I could hear his breath getting louder, faster.

Then he suddenly let go of her. He sat up on the edge of the bed, away from Riva. I couldn't make out any change in her facial expression. She also didn't pull her nightgown back down over her body, but instead remained in the same position until early morning.

File AM217x can be found in the archive folder on Riva and Aston's sexual relationship. It's a sex tape that spread throughout the fan blogs and sports news sites in the second year of their relationship. It's unclear whether it was released as a PR effort or came from a hacker. The video appears equally staged as authentic. It was shot with two cameras and is relatively well lit. At the same time, Aston and Riva are not always entirely recognizable, they move partly out of the frame at times. The video lasts fifteen minutes and shows the entire sexual act. Riva gets things started, she seems playful, but in control. Her facial expression at time code 07:32 stands out in my mind. She keeps her eyes closed and smiles like a Buddhist guru that I saw in a meditation video when I was seven years old. That video also left a lasting impression on me; the image of a person who is naturally at peace with himself and his surroundings.

In the same folder: File KM287a. A papavid™ that doesn't directly have to do with Aston and Riva's relationship, but was given the metatag *sexual content*. The data analyst found it on an obscure society blog. It has only about two hundred thousand likes and was hardly shared. The video shows Riva in the early stages of her professional career, at about thirteen, accompanied by two teammates in a viewtower™ restaurant. The other two were dismissed soon after due to poor results.

The girls are each holding up the same colorful cocktail, they clink glasses at the center of the table, giggle. A clear violation of the rules.

One girl—Mercedes Martinova, according to the facetag—looks around the restaurant. She twists her head around in all directions. Discovers a group of men in their twenties and zeros in on one of them. The men see the invitation and direct all of their attention to the three girls. They send drinks to the table and then come over themselves. Shake the giggling girls' hands. Try to kiss their turned cheeks.

Riva seems younger than the other two, more shy. Her face still looks like a child's face. She hesitates before making space for one of the men next to her, barely answers his questions. She pulls her dress down over her knees.

The picture wobbles when the vj zooms in closer. He concentrates on Riva's face, her lowered eyelids. Does he foresee that Riva will be the one to succeed?

Suddenly, as the video zooms out, the mood changes. The young man puts his hand on Riva's knee again and she doesn't squirm away. He lets his hand drift along her smooth leg, lasered hairless, so that the flysuit™ can rest directly against her skin. A second, improved skin.

Riva maintains her upright posture, continues to participate in the conversation, while his hand crawls up under the fabric, pixelated but discernable in the digital zoom. She laughs.

The camera remains in the static shot until Riva gets up from the table, the man on her arm, and parts ways with the rest of the group. Then the camera follows the two of them along the hotel corridor. Their reflection is multiplied in the floor to ceiling mirrors; they are already tightly wrapped around each other.

The vj's reflection can be seen in the frame here. He maintains some distance as the two book a room at reception and then playfully run to the elevator with the keycard. Riva seems to have a spring in her step, full of anticipation.

The vj loses them behind the closing elevator doors and the video cuts off.

As I click my way through the growing number of files on the server, I suddenly feel lost, as if I'm navigating uncharted waters. What if I miss the essential thing, always looking at a fragment of truth while never grasping its meaning? The more information I gather about Riva, the less sure I am of how to approach my research. There aren't enough clear indications of a sudden psychological break and simultaneously too many potential hypotheses to pursue.

The thought of failure makes me blush. I look around the room, even though I know there's no one here.

I remember how nervous I was when I went into Masters's office for my interview. Seeing him in the middle of the room on all fours, hands and feet on the floor, his butt sticking up in the air in downward dog. His body short, thin, and wiry, as if a life-sized action figure had turned out too small. Masters follows a strict training plan every day in order to counteract his predisposition towards a schoolboy physique.

—Mindfulness training, he said without lifting his head or changing position when he heard me come in. We recommend it to all of our employees. I'll upload the program to your activity tracker when we decide on you.

His words were a relief. The tone was authoritative, as if the decision had been made in my favor long ago. And in spite of my lack of experience in the field of data analysis and my short curriculum vitae. The director of the business academy had recommended me personally.

Masters moved continuously throughout the conversation. Sitting in his office chair, bobbing back and forth. His legs vibrated from constant tiny movements. His left hand drummed on his thigh. Every sixty seconds, he glanced at his fat-burn and heart-rate tracker. According to his fitness profile in the employee database, Masters burns more calories while sitting than others while walking.

When we shook hands to say goodbye, I tried to imitate his pressure exactly.

—A firm handshake, Masters said. I love it.

When I left his office, I could feel the future in my fingertips. The career I had prepared for. The anticipated credit score.

I had the shameful, absurd urge to contact my biomother. To send her a link to the listing on the employee website and the signed contract. *Are you proud of me?*

Archive No.: PMa1
File Type: Urgent-Message™
Sender: @PsySolutions_ID5215d
Recipient: @dancerofthesky

Riva!
You're bored. You can't even stand the view from your apartment window anymore. You want new stimuli. You want a change. But you don't know how. I would like to help you.

4

Aston arrives on time for the onboarding and case history. I observe his gait as he walks from the entrance area to reception. His brief interaction with the receptionist. She gestures her arm towards the elevator and tells him which floor to go to. He's wearing a jacket over a plain v-neck T-shirt and faded jeans, a combination he also wears at small art openings. For larger events, he is outfitted by a style consultant who is known for his unpredictability; anything is possible, from ironically wearing a black turtleneck sweater with a beret to couture designed specifically for the occasion. At his first big opening for Dancer_of_the Sky™, Aston showed up in a dragon costume made of terry cloth. The picture made it into the headlines on most society blogs. Aston as a light-green stuffed dragon, Riva giggling beside him in her designer dress. Beauty and the beast.

Aston stands in the back left corner of the empty elevator.

He looks around, leans back against the wall, and slides down to the floor. He seems to have forgotten about the cameras. He remains crouched, his hands folded over his head, his elbows resting on his knees. He doesn't get up again until the elevator dings at the right floor. Slowly standing, vertebra by vertebra, like the end of a yoga exercise. This is the first time that I have observed such behavior in Aston. A clear gesture of despair and helplessness.

It makes me think of Andorra. How she started trembling in the elevator at the childcare institute, her back pressed up against the wall, suddenly overcome by the fear of us getting stuck. She was afraid of earthquakes and other natural disasters, downright obsessed with news articles about typhoons and floods. They were organized on her tablet by type of catastrophe and the number of dead and injured. Although her collection proved that the most serious and highest frequency of earthquakes occur in the peripheries, Andorra would not let go of her fear. She regularly talked about a scenario that haunted her, that she couldn't escape: Both of us in the elevator at the institute, we had just gotten on at the thirty-fourth floor. Then, a sudden jerk, the cabin stops. A silver metal box dangling on wire ropes over a 300-foot drop. Swaying back and forth, alone.

Aston's behavior suggests that he's more nervous than expected. His short responses to my request to meet sounded nonchalant and came quickly, without much thought. Now that he's inside the building, he may be worried that he's betraying Riva by meeting me. He hasn't told her anything about our appointment. That was his decision.

When Aston steps out of the elevator, he regains his composure. He doesn't look around, but instead walks straight towards therapy room 9, as if he had internalized the building plan. He knocks twice, I call him in.

His handshake is firm. He immediately sits in the therapy chair and doesn't reciprocate my smile. I start the conference call. Aston greets Masters and Beluga Ganz on the monitors with a nod. Whenever he has to sit in on a meeting, Masters prefers videoconferencing to coming down three floors and sitting directly in the room. He claims that it improves the quality of the conversation if the therapist is the only person that the client has to deal with directly. I often wonder how quickly clients start to ignore the monitors during conversations and focus their attention on me alone.

—Thank you for coming.

Aston's facial expression still doesn't reveal a specific attitude towards me or the situation.

—We asked you to join us today, I say, using the standard opening from the inquiry procedure guidelines, to talk to you about your partner Riva Karnovsky's current condition.

Again, Aston does not react to my smile.

I wait a moment to see if he wants to say something and then continue speaking in order to avoid any unpleasant pauses.

—We want to help you help Riva. Our main aim is to provide Riva with the support she needs to find her way out of this acute stress situation—her crisis. We're worried about her.

—Who is we?

Considering our communication thus far, I would not have expected such a confrontational attitude from Aston. His facial expression is aggressive. He looks me right in the eye. In his messages, he seemed polite and cooperative. I got the impression that he was thankful for the invitation.

—Hitomi Yoshida, I say, holding my hand out to him again.

He shakes it briefly. I smile as agreeably as possible.

—PsySolutions has been working with people like Riva for decades. If you help us, we can promise you that she'll get better soon.

—Who is we?

Aston's posture seems tense. His voice sounds strained, the repetition of the sentence has something combative to it. I try to keep my tone as harmless and friendly as possible.

—This is Hugo M. Masters, head of the sports psychology department, and this is Beluga Ganz from quality assurance.

Ganz nods to Aston, Masters seems to be elsewhere with his thoughts.

—We all want to help Riva, I say. Riva's fans are worried, just like your fans would be worried if you suddenly stopped taking pictures.

—And Riva's fans hired you?

I glance at Masters's monitor from the corner of my eye. His facial expression is neutral. He doesn't look back at me.

—Not directly, no. The request comes from the academy. But we see it as a direct reaction to thousands of requests from fans.

Again, I glance at Masters, which Aston notices and follows. Masters hints at a nod.

—Dom Wu hired you?

Aston poses his question to Masters.

—He's one of our contacts at the academy, yes, I say quickly.

Since Masters doesn't react, Aston turns to me again.

—Dom didn't tell me about it, he says.

I sense uncertainty. A reorganization of the situation.

—Obviously, Riva's not talking to anyone about what happened right now, I say. But talking helps, it's that simple. If we can get Riva to confide in you or Dom, she has a chance of getting better.

—What do you mean, what happened? What did happen? What do you know about what happened?

Although he sounds angry, Aston's questions already seem less hostile to me.

—That's exactly what it's about, finding out what happened, I say. We suspect that a critical life event was the trigger. An unfortunate turn of fate, if you will. Do you have any idea what that might have been?

Aston doesn't respond.

Judging from my observations, I consider him emotionally stable. The episode in the elevator is the first sign that Riva's crisis is also weighing on him. On most days, he works ten to sixteen hours in his studio. Initially, with Riva's resignation and the subsequent loss of his biggest project, he seemed artistically blocked. However, he has since acquired several new projects. As far as his output is concerned, he finds himself, apparently, in a highly creative period. From the corner of my eye, I can see Masters's head moving.

—Aston, I say, you're in a very difficult situation. You're on your own. We want to help you.

—I thought you wanted me to help you.

—This is not about us at all. It's about Riva. Riva and you.

I see Masters nodding and I continue to speak.

—Did you know that the Chinese word for crisis is made up of the characters for danger and opportunity? A crisis is an opportunity for change, Aston.

—Are you Chinese?

—No.

The question seems so absurd to me that I let out little chuckle. From the corner of my eye, I notice Masters's facial muscles stiffen. At my employment interview he pointed out several times how important it was to him that his employees follow the inquiry procedure guidelines down to the smallest detail. Open emotional reactions like laughter are completely unacceptable. That is, unless the client laughs first.

—Riva's in a severe depressive phase, I say. As far as we can tell from outside, her condition has deteriorated considerably over the past few days. She is currently unable to seek out help for herself, to trust herself. You are closest to Riva, she trusts you. We can help you strengthen that trust.

Aston's eyes are on the floor. He shrugs and shakes his head. Within a few minutes, his body language has changed from aggressive defensiveness to helplessness. I sense that he is letting go of his inner resistance. During my training, this was called a breaking point: the moment when a previously uncooperative subject begins to recognize the superior role of the therapist.

For most clients, the situation doesn't even get that far. Even when it comes to compulsory therapy sessions, the subjects are largely cooperative. I'm repeatedly surprised by how open and earnest my Call-a-Coach™ clients can be when revealing the details of their situation to me. It's important to them that I have all the information I need to make an informed judgment. When they conceal things, they usually don't do so deliberately, but out of an inability to select, to classify. I listen and sort the fragments of their past into different columns: important, possibly important, unimportant. Finding his work performance strained by his numerous romantic affairs, a man in his mid-fifties once listed off all of the women in his life to me by name. There were fifty-three women. I let him talk and wrote down every one of them. Over the course of several follow-up conversations, I crossed out those he didn't mention again. In the end, three names remained. He was completely surprised by this result and thanked me effusively, as if I had freed him from the burden of responsibility towards the other women.

—Riva is contractually obligated to attend coaching sessions upon her resignation, so that we can determine whether she is unable to work, I say. If she continues to refuse to respond to our invitations, we will be forced to take action.

—What kind of action?

Aston looks up at me.

—Compulsory medications. Relocation. You won't be able to keep the apartment for long.

—She won't leave the house. She won't show up at the sessions.

—Then we'll do it over video. Or audio. That's not a problem.

—She won't pick up.

—Then take the call for her. Support Riva.

—How do you imagine that? Aston asks.

He seems ready to listen now.

—We'll work together, I say. I'll help you deal with Riva and you can answer our questions.

Aston nods almost imperceptibly.

—Have there been any changes in your or Riva's life in the recent weeks and months? For example, did you fight?

—Not really, Aston says. Maybe she's been a bit different than usual.

—What makes you say that?

—The last time there was an accident on a diving show, it was a younger colleague that Riva knew well. When the news came out that she hadn't survived, Riva laughed and said: I would be happy.

—I would be happy?

—Yes. In the sense of: I wish I could have an accident, too.

—Did you dig any deeper?

—I didn't think she meant it.

When I get back to the floor where my office is located, Masters intercepts me in the hallway.

—How far along are you with the document analysis? he asks.

—I'm making some headway. The analyst isn't done with the data mining yet.

—Put more pressure on him.

Masters's tie knot is crooked. He must have loosened it for a moment and then forgotten to tighten it again. I consider whether I should point it out.

—There are fifty-eight hours until the deadline for the as-is analysis, Masters says, as if he were reading the data.

I nod.

—In order to take the necessary course of action, we need full cooperation from Karnovsky's partner, he adds. And don't laugh again. During a client interview, I mean. It undermines your authority. You don't want to appear insecure.

I nod. Masters moves sideways past me in the direction of his office. From behind, you can't see his crooked tie, he looks neat and tidy, easily interchangeable in his dark-blue virgin wool suit. I imagine him between meetings, his office door closed as he leans back in his chair and loosens his tie to take four deep breaths.

As soon as I upload the meeting minutes onto the securecloud™, Masters immediately starts making corrections. With each revision, I feel a sharp sting, as if his notes were being written with a needle on my body.

5

I like coming back to my apartment. I feel a great sense of pride when I use my key fob and hear the click of the lock along with the clear high-pitched tone that signals its release. My apartment is located in the twenty-fourth district, only four districts away from the first flagship buildings. I've been on the waiting list since I started my training at the business academy. My VIP assignment at PsySolutions is what finally got me in. Every time I walk through the door, I stop on the threshold for a moment and let my eyes wander across my little kingdom, filled with a sense of certainty, assurance that I'm on the right path.

Before I activate my tablet for the evening shift at Call-a-Coach™, I give myself some time to sit on a stool at the kitchen counter and eat a light dinner in my apartment.

I read the news while I eat, occasionally glancing out the window at the lit windows in other buildings. I can do little more than imagine the activity down on the street, since the people and various modes of transport are almost indistinguishable in the dark. At the office tower opposite my apartment, there are always individual floors and units with their lights on at night; apparently, someone is always up working. So far, I haven't been able to recognize a regular pattern—no specific windows where the light shines every night. I notice that this inconsistency makes me nervous. As a child, I would often stare for hours at the apartments across the street that still had their lights on at night. Seeing a lit window would give me a sense of security. I imagined living there and sitting at the table with the people whose silhouettes I could see. Today it feels like an unbridgeable divide. The residents of the other buildings seem like people on screens, pixel formations that exist independently of real bodies.

I usually do the evening meditation sessions from my mindfulness program seated at the kitchen counter with my eyes open. I like the way the world outside slowly blurs at the moment of relaxation, the way my gaze turns inward. How, instead of the hum of the air conditioning, I can hear the inside of my ears. It sounds like the sea, even though I know it's just my blood circulation.

The last time I was by the sea was as a child. Every year we went with the institute to the same resort, there were several pools and a beach with grayish-white sand. The other children preferred the pools, the clear chlorinated water, the slides and diving boards. For some unknown reason, I was drawn to the sea. Even though it was embarrassing for me, I would go to the beach alone every day. I would sit hidden in a corner right next to the barrier and look out at the water.

I use this memory in my visualization exercises. Once the meditation app has started and is playing its even, metronome-like rhythm, I think about the beach. Just like I did then, I observe the sea with its complicated wave formations, its constantly breaking surface. The white foam, the algae and driftwood like sea creatures reaching out of the water from a distance.

Andorra was the only one who ever came over from the pool and sat next to me from time to time. For several minutes, we would sit there cross-legged, so close that our knees touched. But sitting always got too boring for her, she wanted to go into the water. I sometimes let myself be persuaded, but regretted it every time. As soon as I was immersed in it, the sea lost everything that was sublime about it; it was suddenly cold, salty, and dirty. It would cling to me for hours, even after I had thoroughly washed my skin and hair.

The meditation isn't working for me. My thoughts digress. Riva invades my mind, how she stubbornly sits on the floor of her apartment and refuses to speak, to explain herself, to eat, to drink. I see her slender figure losing substance. I see her becoming porous, her skeleton shines through beneath her clothes and skin.

I try to concentrate on my calming place. Riva appears like a pixelated shadow next to me on the beach. So close that I can feel the tenseness in her body. Her tension spreads to me like a virus.

I try to physically shake it off, shifting back and forth on my chair to find my balance. Then I restart the app, start the exercise from the beginning, but my thoughts drift off again, unwanted images force their way in. I can't manage to let go of them.

I go over tonight's to-do list. In ninety-five minutes I have a date with a man who was recommended to me by a partnering agency. It doesn't scare me to meet a potential partner, but I'm annoyed about the date right now. I'm not in the right mood. My head hurts, I feel wound up. It'll be obvious that my meditation was unsuccessful.

I consider writing him to cancel. But the agency counts cancellations as negative points in your profile if you don't link to a doctor's note. I haven't exchanged many messages with the man yet; I can't think of his screen name, but the profile that the partnering agency created from his personal data seemed likeable to me, solid. Like me, he put in the effort to complete the automatically generated profile and fill in any gaps. In the *Particulars* section, he mentioned a dislike of anything supernatural, which appealed to me. I couldn't enter into a relationship with an esoteric or superstitious person.

The things we talked about in our short, moderated chats were mainly of an administrative nature: the timing of the first meeting according to our work hours, our sexual preferences, and general ideas about sexual intercourse. The exchange of our STD tests and sterilization certificates. Our preferences regarding gifts.

A long-term partnership has been recommended to us as the goal of the relationship, but without a shared living space. Individual independence is at the top of our respective lists of values.

I start the meditation app again. I take a deep breath and let the contours of my apartment blur before my eyes. I return to my calming place once more, imagine the sea, the sand, the sound of the seagulls.

I feel a person beside me again. Hopefully it's Andorra this time. Her childhood form often appears in my visualizations. She intensifies my feeling of security. When I turn to her, it's Riva looking back at me, looking through me as if I weren't there. When we were kids, Andorra sometimes looked at me that way.

I asked her what she was thinking about one time.

—Nothing, she said. About you, how I talk to you.

I suspected that she was lying, that her mouth had just been babbling and her brain had been focused on something completely different. Maybe a boy.

—Don't lie to me, I said.

Andorra was popular among the boys at the institute.

And it wasn't just because she was beautiful with her perfectly symmetrical face and thick black hair that she twisted into countless little braids every morning. Wherever she went, that's where all the attention was focused, even when it came to the adults. The educators often accused her of staging the small dramatic scenes that always took place around her. Her exuberant energy seemed to transmit like electricity. I also felt infected by her thirst for action. Without Andorra, I probably would have had a very boring childhood without even noticing it.

But the older we got, the more I realized how different we were. How differently we were treated. While the others at the institute hardly exchanged a word with me, Andorra's mere presence provoked extreme reactions. Some kids would scramble for a chance to talk or play with her, they'd scratch her name into the walls of the toilet stalls. Others hid from her. The fact that some children were afraid of her, Andorra learned from me.

—Someone in the bathroom told me that you were planning a murder and that last year you beat up Bentley in the utility closet, I said.

We lay next to each other in her bed that night and whispered.

—That's not true, Andorra said.

—I know.

Andorra and I often slept in the same bed. We would chat quietly until Andorra's eyes started closing. I watched as she drifted off into the world of sleep. At first, she would twitch as if she were falling. Then her breath got calmer. When she dreamt, her lips moved, and later, if I stayed awake long enough, her eyeballs did their own dance under her eyelids. When she lay there like that, I often stroked her hair and imagined myself as a bio-mother watching over her.

I finally decide to quit the meditation exercise and put my plate in the dishwasher. Now I have more time to prepare for the date than expected. To shower, put on make-up, hair spray, perfume. I already prepared an outfit for myself in the morning, which I slip on quickly after showering. Although I'm basically satisfied with my body, I feel uncomfortable being naked or just in my underwear.

I've chosen a gray-blue suit with a white blouse instead of a dress as a signal that I don't want sexual contact today. It should be a short evening for us to get to know each other a little better, so that we can think about the possibility of a relationship before we arrange to meet again.

The man is also wearing a business outfit, a tailored suit with a white shirt and tie. We smile at each other with a sense of relief. He introduces himself as Royce Hung. We shake hands and then exchange two air kisses on the cheek. He smells good, like a certain designer cologne, but I can't think of the brand. The partnering agency selected the restaurant according to our preferences and we both like it very much. It's a rotating viewtower™ restaurant. Royce makes a comment about the city being beautiful and we clink glasses; he ordered champagne.

To maintain the spontaneous nature of a first date, I usually don't read all of the information in my potential partner's profile. I try to imagine what Royce Hung's profession could be, probably a middle management position at a mid-sized company. Our credit-score levels are similar, as I specified in the placement request.

—What do you do for a living? I ask to get the conversation going.

—Head of public relations for Demi & White.

—The cosmetics company?

—That's the one.

—Do you get a lot of samples? He smiles and nods.

—Next time I'll bring you some. Send me your list.

He refills my glass. I drank too fast and can feel my cheeks turning red.

—And you?

—Business psychologist.

—Ah, he says. I'd rather not have any samples from your job. But that must be an exciting industry.

I laugh to make him feel like he said the right thing.

—Not always, I say. It depends on the client. Can you imagine what it's like to talk to an accountant about how he does his work?

Royce laughs now, too. He has a nice laugh, almost like a bird cooing. It seems to erupt from deep within his body.

I use the line about the accountant as an icebreaker often, even though—or maybe even because—it isn't true. So far, I've only done one live-video analysis of an accountant and it was during my training. I actually enjoyed it very much. I could have watched him enter numbers into spreadsheets for years. As a child, I liked to organize things. I would sort things like bags of different colored plastic beads into little compartments according to color. The repeated thought process and the visible creation of order had a calming effect on me.

—Where did you study? Royce asks.

—Bowen Institute of Business.

—Not bad. No doubt you were one of those overachievers who got an apprenticeship in the city right at the first casting.

—I didn't grow up in the peripheries.

—What?

He looks at me in disbelief. I can see his mind processing the unusual information. I should have lied. It just kind of slipped out. The shame of having made a mistake. I take a big sip of champagne and try to smile.

—Wow, he says. I thought those were rumors. Do your parents work for the government?

—Lobbyists for s&p.

—Did you live with your parents?

—No!

I burst into laughter, which I immediately regret. Alcohol affects my self-control mechanisms. Royce Hung's expression has changed, I can feel the distance growing between us.

—I was in a city home, I say, but my mother visited me sometimes.

My biomother, entering the visitor's area at the institute, always half an hour late because her meeting went over and always talking on her tablet in a hushed indoor voice. Me, standing there, stuffed in a dress picked out especially for the occasion, two bows in my hair, like a gift.

She looks pretty, my mother would always say to the caregiver before coming over to me. She would take a long look at me first and then spread her arms out wide. I had been waiting for this from the moment I was brought into the visitor's area. I would have to hold myself back from leaping into her arms. Instead, I took controlled steps towards her and then slowly leaned into the physical contact that was being offered. To feel her slender arms wrap around me. At this point, the caregiver had already left the room. If there were no other visitors, we would be alone. I imagined that we lived together in that room, my mother and I. That she had just come home from work and now the day was really starting. With games and discussions and our own trainings in all my favorite disciplines.

—A city home. That must have cost an unbelievable amount of credits, Royce says into my silence.

I shrug and smile. I wish I could redirect the conversation to another topic, but I sense that his curiosity won't so easily be appeased. It's my own fault.

—But isn't it impossible to get authorization to live in the city without an employment contract? he asks.

—We were all registered with ghost addresses in the peripheries and went to the required castings every six months.

—Surveillance must be aware of things like that.

I laugh again. I'm afraid he might think I'm laughing at him, so I touch his fingertips on the table.

—Of course surveillance knows. That's why it costs so much, I say in my most confiding tone, my work voice.

His expression encourages me to keep talking.

—As soon as the parents can't afford it anymore, they're busted. I've seen a few kids get taken away from one day to the next. And then, because of the criminal proceedings, they and their parents don't make it back. I don't think my biomother was aware of the risk at the beginning. She often regretted it and was very afraid that she would have to go back to the peripheries. She never forgave me for that.

—That means you have contact with your bioparents?

—With my mother. But rarely.

I can't quite remember the last time I heard my biomother's voice. In my memory, it blends together with the voice of her assistant. *She's in a meeting. But I'll let her know.*

—I can't imagine what it's like, Royce says. To know your bioparents.

—It's actually nothing special. You just have better career opportunities if you grew up in the city. But you seem to have managed anyway.

He laughs, we laugh together, we've found a rhythm. Our fingertips touch in the middle of the table. I almost regret having put on the suit and not the dress. But I don't like changing my plans.

The rules of a successful date dictate that it's now Royce's turn. I ask him questions about the beginning of his career, his first casting experience. To talk about his LCM™, the life-changing-moment™ when he was finally allowed to stay on stage until the very end, when he got accepted into a city academy. About the size of his apartment and the prestige of the districts where he's lived. And finally, about his work, his responsibilities, the VIPs he works with.

I try to concentrate on him, on his short, efficient sentences, never a syllable too many. But I notice myself drifting inward, my thoughts wandering back to the visitor's area at the institute, to the silence before the door opens and my mother appears. Before she opens her arms and I can lean into them.

Royce kisses me before I get into the cab. It's a short, pleasant kiss. His skin is freshly shaven and soft, his lips are thin but warm. In the car, I can't help but smile in the dark and nestle into the upholstery as if it were a person.

Archive No.: PMa2
File Type: Urgent-Message™
Sender: @PsySolutions_ID5215d
Recipient: @dancerofthesky

Riva!
You're desperate. When one of your colleagues has an
accident, you catch yourself thinking: I would be happy
to trade places. But think of the little girl you once were.
Imagine her, lonely and lost in the peripheries. Think of
the dust and the heat. The sweat on her forehead. The dirt
sticking to that sweat. Remember how you wanted nothing
more than to finally be clean. The child you once were—
what would she say to you now if she could see you like this,
on the floor in your luxury apartment, idle. What would she
do? She would shake you and beg: Seize the opportunity!
Don't throw away our dream! Please don't send me back
into the dirt and meaninglessness!

Riva, you still haven't attended any of your designated
coaching sessions. This entitles your contract partners to
initiate criminal proceedings against you. Don't you think a
better solution would be to reach out for the hand being
offered and accept help?

6

The city unfolding. Its crisscrossing bridges, one over the other, maze-like, while simultaneously regulating and directing traffic. The cars, rolling onward at a constant speed, maintaining a regular distance from each other, going their separate ways at the intersections, and finding their way back into the steady flow of traffic a moment later. Neatly strung together like beads. At the major intersection that is visible from my office, there are eight feeder roads. The highest one almost reaches the middle levels of the neighboring skyscrapers. The bridges wind in all directions, oval, figure eight, and then straight ahead again.

I follow each path with my eyes, an exercise in attentiveness. At the end, I return to the main road, which almost runs straight through the entire city as a line of sight, a bottleneck.

The office is buzzing. I don't normally notice the hum of the server towers anymore, as my perceptive faculties have stored it as peripheral background noise. But today my nerves are exposed. I slept poorly. I kept thinking about the date with Royce Hung, going over it in my head, word for word. Looking back, I am increasingly aware of my mistakes, the choice of unapproachable attire, my mention of the city home, the amount of time

I let pass before giving Royce a chance to talk about himself. His evaluation of the date will be poor. He might give me two stars, three at most.

I couldn't stop thinking about the moment he kissed me. The warmth of the taxi on the way home.

I can still feel the night sweat clinging to my skin, despite a shower, freshly washed clothes, and a ventilation system. Since starting this job, I usually reach the recommended sleep time of six hours, but the activity tracker only recorded it as two hundred and fifty-two minutes last night.

I try to concentrate my thoughts on one point, keeping my eyes on one silvery car. I lose sight of it when it drives under a bridge.

The notification beep has been going off on Riva's tablet for thirty seconds. How does she tolerate that sound? Riva is standing at the window and looking out, as if the sound weren't coming from her room but from mine.

After exactly thirty-four seconds, Aston storms into the room. He grabs the tablet and throws it against the wall. One of his photo frames falls to the ground. Riva jumps and turns to him.

—That was the sixth summons, Riva.

—Is it broken?

Aston picks the device up off the floor, taps on it, shakes his head.

—If you don't go, if you don't at least answer, they'll kick us out of the apartment.

I try to see things from Aston's perspective. I choose the camera closest to him and zoom in until I can see over his shoulder. Riva has turned around again and is looking out the window. From this point of view, her body looks like a two-dimensional cardboard figure against the light, a promotional cutout of Riva, like the ones you can buy in online fan shops.

Although I've only been observing her for a little over a week, the image on the monitor has already shaped my entire perception of Riva. I can't reconcile the news videos and papavids™ in my data archive, the pictures of Riva outside, in the air, in bars and restaurants, with the woman at the window. No connection seems to exist between them, even if they resemble each other on the surface. None of the saved video interviews show any indications of discontent. Just two days before breaking her contract, Riva was still appearing on video chat with fans. She makes jokes and laughs, answers questions according to her personal brand.

Only in one single interview two weeks before her resignation was there a sort of scandal. Riva answered a vj's first question with a smile in a practiced, overly sweet tone:

—Am I happy about winning? Can't you think of anything more original? Do you only ask questions that you could answer yourself? I think winning is shit, to be honest. Fuck winning.

Dom dragged her out of the press zone by the arm. Just a few minutes later, the video had already been shared and edited millions of times, fuck-winning songs, fuck-winning T-shirts, fuck-winning ringtones. It was rumored that it might have been planned as a viral marketing campaign by the academy.

—A psychologist, Aston says, sent you three messages.

He has picked up Riva's tablet and is scrolling through her unread messages.

—You could go there at least once to see what it's like. You have to talk to someone.

New files are displayed on my work monitor. Entries

on a fan blog by the user @gokarnovsky. Pictures and lists of things he or she found in Riva's trashcan. Hashtag: *flirtedwiththegarbageman*.

The lists were uploaded over a period of two weeks. @gokarnovsky posted updates every day. There's nothing that particularly stands out in Riva's garbage. Packaging, old backup batteries, a defective charging cable, a half-used lipstick, empty medicine packs. Nutritional water bottles. Fruit shot and muscle bar wrappers. I assume that the food packaging came from Aston.

Nine days have passed since the start of the project. According to the timetable, the basic data analysis should have been complete within eight days, along with the first steps towards subject rehabilitation. In my performance reviews, Masters's tone has changed. I no longer open them as soon as they appear in the notification window. I am less and less able to shake my feelings of inadequacy or transform my self-doubt into motivation for my work, which is what I advise my clients to do. Even though I make every effort to implement Masters's feedback as well and as quickly as possible, his comments become more negative. On the ratings portals, his leadership strategy is described as being non-invasive and focused on positive reinforcement. I wonder if I am the only one he criticizes this harshly. Whether I have to regard myself as an anomaly. Whether I am noticeably worse than my colleagues.

During my studies, I wrote a whitepaper analyzing the advantages and disadvantages of employee leaderboards and comparison platforms. I argued that the motivational effects of the objective workplace performance ranking far exceeded the risk of potential discouragement in the event of poor results. Without the impetus to advance in the rankings through improved output, employees are less productive. Company studies have shown, I wrote, that data-based and therefore highly objective competition improves employee performance.

I make an effort to see Masters's feedback as constructive; to be grateful, even if the criticism hits me as a surprise. He accuses me of following arbitrary impulses in my research. During my job interview, he praised me specifically for my intuitive therapeutic approach. In the course of the recruitment process, he had listened to and even listened in on many of my Call-a-Coach™ consultations. I was impressed by the fact that he had gotten a hold of the confidential recordings. PsySolutions is well known for its good contacts in private companies across all industries.

—A major challenge with this job, Masters said during the interview, is sticking to the inquiry procedure guidelines while also reacting spontaneously to the situation.

Since the job began, however, he has only insisted on standardization and systematization. *Your logs are too confusing,* he wrote in my last review. *More visualizations! Use the graphics department. We have to present investors with something they understand at a glance. We need an idea of how things are going to proceed!*

Sometimes I'm afraid that my data archive is showing a version of Riva that is no longer alive and can't be revived. Riva, as she exists now, has become one with her apartment: a white, motionless figure. More outline than person. Riva the high-rise diver seems like fiction to me. What I see on the live monitor is Riva without characteristics, without goals. In the archive data or in the present, I can't find any indications of an injury that would justify her state.

How we wished for a life like hers, Andorra and I.

When we sat there between the other children, bobbing up and down with excitement in front of our monitors for half an hour before the livestream even began. We couldn't bear to miss a second of the castings for high-rise diving™. Then, finally, the familiar scene, backstage in the wings, the curtain from behind. Legs, fidgeting restlessly on the spot. The glare of the spotlight. A blurry girl's figure in a pink tutu. We hummed along to the intro music, drumming the beat on our legs. The moderator steps up to the microphone: Welcome to *Casting Queens*™.

Andorra and I shared one *Casting Queens*™ fan T-shirt. We took turns sleeping in it. Andorra sometimes held a judging in one of the bedrooms, standing on the bed.

—Line up in a row. Number 7, you're out, you looked like a shriveled balloon. Disappointing. Number 23, your performance was good, but you have no presence, no star quality, look how you stand with your shoulders slumped. And Number 3, what kind of clothes are you wearing, your caregiver wouldn't be able to pick you out of a line-up if her life depended on it.

Old episodes of the show played non-stop on the flat screen in the lounge; nobody wanted to watch anything else. There's an episode with Riva, but I don't remember her standing out to me back then.

Why would anyone voluntarily give up such a life? My first theory was that it had to be a physical trigger, a hormonal impairment. But Riva's medical data doesn't show any of the values that are indicative of such a change. Her vital score index™ was high, very high, at every required examination. Her performance level was hindered a few times by harmless infectious diseases that were passed around the academy and couldn't be eliminated immediately. In her first year, she fell into the training net several times and once broke her arm, but both Dom Wu and Riva's academy doctor have officially confirmed to me that there were no serious problems with Riva's health prior to her breach of contract.

Aston taps his way through the messages on Riva's tablet.

—At least meet Dom, he says, you owe him that.

Riva goes to the kitchen and pours herself a drink. You can hear ice cubes clattering against glass. She looks over at Aston.

—If it'll make you happy, she says.

She takes small sips of her drink. Gin. If she consumes any liquid at all, it's usually hard alcohol. Before she quit, she would mostly only drink alcohol to promote her signature cocktail the flydive™.

Now she is standing at the window again, so close that her breath is fogging up the glass. The server tower fan starts up. I click my way through the already viewed video files and archive photos again. Even though they seem purely made up to me at the moment, they still remind me of what this is all about: recovery and the reactivation of lost potential.

I log in to my partnering agency profile to see if Royce Hung has submitted a review of our date yet. There are two new partner suggestions on my start page. I click them away without opening them. Royce hasn't written a review or a message, his last login was the afternoon before our date. He's probably delaying his feedback. I myself wait at least two days before I write a review, so that I have a more objective view of the meeting and can be a hundred percent sure of my comments.

7

My work rhythm isn't ideal. When I'm not sitting at the monitor, I feel like I'm missing something important. Every time I return to the office, I scroll through the log of the previous minutes or hours first. I can only concentrate on the present once I've gone through whatever I missed.

I try to adapt my day-night rhythm to Riva's rhythm, but it's irregular. Some days, she's already up at 4 a.m. On others, she doesn't fall asleep until early in the morning and then stays in bed until noon. On the night-vision videos, I often see her walking in a circle in the living room for several minutes.

I sent Aston prescriptions for sleeping pills and sedatives several times and asked him to motivate Riva to take them. According to his financial reports, he picked up the medication, though he hasn't spoken to Riva about it yet.

My activity tracker reads 1:17 a.m. I should've been asleep an hour ago. Lying in bed on my back, the room filled with hazy gray light, I picture Riva in her bed, how she lies with her arms and legs stretched out to the sides, eyes on the ceiling. Her skin, suddenly covered in sweat—a phenomenon that often occurs alongside sleep issues as they interfere with the body's ability to regulate temperature. Her formerly muscular body is flaccid, broken down.

I wonder at what point the loss of muscle mass will reach a level where rehabilitation is no longer viable. How much time I have left.

The earliest recording of Riva that the analyst could find was from a general casting. It's not even certain that it's really her. Her first name appears in the video tag, but there's an unknown last name. Riva is six years old at most, smaller than the other girls in her age category. She looks into the camera, unsure. Her body is tense, her neck stiff. She competes in different categories and is not particularly good in any of them.

She still draws attention, stands out. When all the other children have left, she stays on stage. The announcement is made twice in a polite but firm tone. All candidates are asked to leave the stage. She doesn't react. She stands there, motionless, mute. In the same way that adult Riva sits on the floor of her apartment.

The difference is that Riva doesn't seem stubborn in the recording from the casting. Her figure, frozen in place, doesn't manifest as resistance. It's as if she forgot where she was and what she should do. As if she had temporarily lost control over her body. I wonder if that's also the case now. Should she just be told what to do over a loudspeaker?

Riva, the voice in the video finally says, probably after finding her name on the list of candidates. Riva, please step off the stage so the next group can perform. And Riva, suddenly awake again, walks off the stage. Shortly afterwards, the jingle sounds and the first candidate from the next group comes on stage. In the close-up, you can see her lower lip trembling.

My eyes burn and feel puffy. I've already taken three

sleeping pills. According to the package insert, that's the absolute maximum. I can't stop thinking about Riva, the deadline, the next steering committee meeting, how there will be more material to sift through in the archive folder by morning. I half-heartedly do relaxation exercises that only wear me out more. I get up at half-hour intervals and walk around my apartment.

At 3:17 a.m., I click on a parentbot app. As is required by my contract, I use a scrambler in addition to the usual security measures. Regardless, I still feel uneasy about being identified by voice-analysis software during the conversation.

—Hello, my darling, the bot says.

I've chosen the mother option. It simulates a woman around fifty years old. Her voice has a warm, deep tone and a calm, almost sedate cadence.

—Hello.

—What's the matter, darling?

I'm always surprised by how quickly you forget you're talking to a machine during the conversation. The voice and ability to respond are practically indistinguishable from actual human beings. For my final thesis paper, I investigated the phenomenon under worse technical conditions. Even then, after just a few seconds, the test subjects showed signs of basic trust, similar to that felt towards a friend. Even if they deliberately concentrated on the fact that they were talking to a bot once a minute and used the memory function on their tablets. Even then, they would forget about it from one minute to the next.

—I can't sleep, I say.

—I'm sorry to hear that. Did you try taking a sleeping pill?

—Yes.

—Are you thinking about something in particular that's keeping you awake?

—My work.

The voice at the other end laughs.

—Then you're working too hard again, my dear.

—I'm stuck.

—You don't have to get anywhere at this second.

—That's true.

—I'm proud of you, whether or not you make any progress, the voice says.

I let her words resonate in me. I feel a little better already. Maybe, if I talk to her for a while, I'll be able to fall asleep after all.

—But you can't stop thinking about it? she asks when I don't respond.

—I can't stop thinking about it.

—Would it help to talk about it?

—I think so.

For a moment I listen to the silence on the line, then I say:

—She makes me angry.

—Who?

—My subject. She shouldn't make me angry, but she makes me angry.

The mother makes a sound confirming she has heard, understood. I'm happy to hear her voice. At night, along with the darkness, I often feel like there's an audio filter between me and my surroundings. Suddenly, it's as if I'm the only person left in the world. The muffled sounds I hear through the walls and ceiling of my apartment seem like apparitions, an echo of the dead. The quiet whirring of the cooling wall. A vibrating hum in the walls. Mechanical clicking. The only times I feel connected to the living again are when my tablet rings and I hear the voice of a client on the line.

—It doesn't make sense, I say, that such a successful woman, known for her desire to perform, suddenly throws away everything she's earned.

—I understand, the voice says, which sounds a bit like my own mother, if I remember correctly.

Only the vocal timbre is different, more attentive.

We've drifted apart, my biomother said, before she stopped responding to my calls and messages. My high scores never really impressed her; she seemed to object to something more fundamental about me that I could never figure out.

I had hoped you would progress further, she said in our last conversation. That you would do more with your life, considering it came at such a high premium.

—A life at such a high premium, I say to the bot.

—Life is valuable, the voice answers, you're right, my darling. Life is the most valuable thing we have.

And what if it's an actual woman talking to me? What if someone is sitting in a dark room at the other end of the line? Someone who really cares about me?

—What exactly are you angry about? the woman asks.

—I'm not sure, I say. Maybe it's that she's ungrateful. A defiant child, who has been given a lollipop, but throws it on the ground because it's not the right flavor. You want to shake her and scream that things have never been as good as they are today.

—You're right, the bot says. I am glad that you've grown into such a reasonable woman. What did I always tell you as a child? We should consider ourselves lucky.

—Yes, mom, I say, exactly. We should consider ourselves lucky.

The conversation has calmed me down. My body feels warmer and heavier than before. I go back to bed and try a visualization exercise to ease the transition to sleep. I imagine lying in my bed at the childcare institute. Although I know that my memories are unreliable, my memory of the bedroom at the institute seems as clear and real as a virtual-reality projection.

I look around the room, our double bedroom. I hear Andorra quietly breathing next to me. She's lying on her side, facing me. Her hand hangs from the bed, just above the floor, an appendage forgotten in sleep. I reach for it, gently hold it, bring it up to my eye. I look at the tiny lines in her skin, her fingerprints, run my finger over them.

—Hey, Andorra says and pulls her hand back, what are you doing with my hand, you pervert?

It makes me laugh. What are you doing, I repeat quietly in my bed in my apartment. I see Andorra's face, the creased imprint from her pillow. Her feigned anger, the theatrically raised eyebrows. What are you doing to me while I sleep? Andorra shaking her head and jumping from her bed over to mine. She jumps on the bed until she's tired and then falls asleep next to me. I laugh at myself for holding my friend's hand while she sleeps. I don't dare touch her when she's awake, when she's loud and jumping. Not in this way.

Archive No.: PMa3
File Type: Urgent-Message™
Sender: @PsySolutions_ID5215d
Recipient: @dancerofthesky

Riva!
You still haven't complied with any of our six obligatory meeting requests.
You're not just abandoning yourself this way, but also the

people who've always been there for you. Your breach of contract puts Dom Wu and the academy in a precarious situation. Dom is very worried about you. He doesn't understand why you won't tell him what's going on.

Remember when you came to the academy as a little girl. Remember how lonely you were in those big spacious rooms. Your fear of failure. Of being sent back. And how Dom made you feel like you weren't alone. How he patiently explained every training unit, every diving form to you. Don't you also owe an explanation to the people who invested their time and love in you?

Don't just throw away what you've worked so hard for. If you don't do it for yourself, at least do it for Dom and Aston.

8

—Ms. Yoshida.

I notice the changes as soon as I enter Masters's office. A single potted plant in the middle of the otherwise empty desk. All electronic devices have disappeared, no monitors, no servers, no cables. There also seems to be less furniture. As far as I can remember, in addition to the desk and two armchairs, there were previously also several shelves, small tables, and decorative items.

Hugo M. Masters is standing at the window, against the light.

—Digital cleanse, the shadowy silhouette says.

All of the sockets are covered with electrical tape. The room is silent, no humming, only Masters's breath and his voice.

—Computers are fucking exhausting, Masters says. I've been feeling better ever since I put all that crap in my assistant's office. You should also engage more intensively with the mindfulness principles, Ms. Yoshida. That would be good for you.

I nod. He signals for me to sit in one of the chairs. He stays standing in front of me, observing me.

—What gets you out of bed in the morning, Ms. Yoshida?

—What do you mean by that?

—What drives you? What's your favorite thing to do? What's your passion?

—Psychology?

—The mere fact that you formulate your answer as a question shows me that psychology is not your passion. Why did you choose this profession?

The truth is: because I got a high score in the area of business psychology on the institute's aptitude test.

What do you think you're going to wind up doing, Andorra once asked me. We were sitting on the roof of the institute building. Andorra was sprawled out on the concrete, nothing between her and the unfiltered sun. I was sitting under a UV screen and looking over at her, my legs pulled up against my body. The concrete roof was stained and uneven. Small rain puddles had collected in several places.

—I don't know, I said. My scores in economics and math are in the upper range. I'll probably get accepted at the business academy.

—And what about diving?

—I don't have the scores for that.

A pigeon landed near us. It drank from one of the puddles and then climbed all the way in, so that its legs disappeared into the water.

—I'll probably get accepted at a business academy, too, Andorra said.

—Then we'll study together.

—But I have no interest in business.

The pigeon stood motionless in the rainwater. It watched us as if it understood every word.

—The pigeon is eavesdropping, I said.

Andorra looked over at it and posed as if the pigeon were taking a picture of her.

—You can't always have what you want, I said. For diving we would have to have been enrolled at a sports academy long ago.

Andorra turned away from me to face the sun. She had her eyes closed.

—We have to go back down again.

Andorra didn't move from her reclined position on the concrete. The pigeon took a few steps out of the puddle and flew away as if it were responding to what I had said.

I went over to Andorra, put my hand on her shoulder.

She opened her eyes and sat up.

—Doesn't it make you angry, she asked, that we can't decide anything for ourselves?

—They're just trying to identify and foster our potential. You can still say no.

—Who do you know that has ever said no?

—But they don't force you.

Andorra's blouse was dusty from lying with her back on the concrete. I patted the dirt off of her.

—They just show us the best possible version of ourselves, I said.

—Are you sure about that?

I wonder what kind of answer Masters wants to hear. Maybe he would be impressed if I said: I'm a business psychologist because I have good opportunities for advancement and the prospect of a high salary.

I've taken too long to answer. Masters looks at me disapprovingly.

—In the recruitment process, two things about you impressed me, he says. One was your ability to instantly assess people over an audio connection without needing more intimate access to them. I've listened to some of your Call-a-Coach™ consultations. It was a little like watching an animal tamer, the way you brought those people from an emotional excitement level of ten down to a five in a very short time. I remember one case in particular. A level-three manager. Such a classic upper-level manager, quickly rising in the ranks, on the fast track to becoming an executive. A real go-getter. I immediately recognized his vocal pitch, the precise, levelheaded way in which he put every word in the right place, even at the moment when he had hit rock bottom. At the absolute low point of his life. He still retained something authoritative, a fundamental self-confidence. He impressed me. I wondered if I would show the same incisiveness in his situation.

Masters's eyes are still pointed in my direction, but his gaze seems to go straight through me.

—When you accepted the call, the man said: I have a gun pointed at my head and a noose around my neck. All I have to do is jump off the chair or pull the trigger. But I can't decide which way to die. And then, in the same matter-of-fact tone, you said: Then we'll make a pros and cons list together. Ha! Do you remember?

—Of course I remember.

—You immediately knew it would work.

—Yes.

—That impressed me.

—Thank you.

—Of course, you were operating under the assumption that a suicidal person has already decided against suicide the moment he reaches for the tablet.

—Not necessarily.

—I, for one, wouldn't have expected him to let it go. I bought into his air of self-confidence. I thought: If I were him, I would have planned this well in advance and now I would follow through with it.

—Then maybe you would have done it.

—Do you think so?

—I can't say with any certainty.

Masters is silent. He seems to be earnestly considering the question. He's the last person I would suspect of having suicidal tendencies. It's interesting that he identifies so strongly with a man to whom he has no connection other than his professional position.

—Do you know how he's doing today? he asks.

—No.

—You didn't look into it?

—In this case, it was only about acute intervention.

—But weren't you curious?

—He was transferred to a psychiatric institution by company management. It was no longer my responsibility.

—I have to admit that I did some research, Masters says in an almost apologetic tone.

Our conversation dynamics have changed entirely. I feel relaxed, almost cheerful. Never before has Masters been so forthcoming with me.

—It bothered me, you see. I couldn't forget the man's voice. It was easy enough to find him. He's now an executive manager, just as I'd expected. He obviously overcame his little crisis quickly.

—Did it make you feel better to know?

—In a certain way, it did, Masters says. But it really nagged at me that I couldn't at all figure out what motivated him. Maybe it was just a substance issue. The wrong dose of medication.

—Possibly.

—But you didn't find anything?

Masters's tone suddenly sounds distant and critical again. I sense that his question is no longer referring to Call-a-Coach™, but Riva Karnovsky instead.

—Mr. Masters, I'm sorry that the data analysis is taking longer than planned. I wouldn't have expected it to be so difficult to determine the stressors. The data doesn't reveal enough information. The psychograph shows no indication of any crisis situations. But I am confident that—

Masters holds his hand up so that I stop talking.

—If we don't deliver within the time frame, the investors will back out, he says.

—I know, Mr. Masters, but we will. I'm close, it won't take much longer. I promise you that I'll deliver results as soon as possible.

The unpleasant feeling I had at the beginning of the conversation is back.

—What was the second thing? I try to redirect the conversation.

—What do you mean?

—You said that you were impressed by two things about me in the recruitment process.

I immediately regret having asked the question. Masters looks at me with an annoyed, distant expression.

—Your article on businesspsychology.corp about the emotional effects of smooth surfaces in architecture, he then says. Decluttering. I liked that. I've already experienced for myself how the sight of a smooth, reflective surface can calm me down. That's one of the reasons why I chose to do a digital cleanse.

He gestures around the room with his arms.

—I'm honored, I say. Masters's face darkens.

—In the Karnovsky case, he says, maybe it's not necessarily the right approach to try to determine the cause of the crisis. You should focus on acute crisis intervention, like in the case with the manager.

—I don't believe that a therapy based purely on acute behavior can lead to long-term reintegration, I say. Especially if the subject doesn't cooperate.

—Then get her to cooperate.

—She's very resistant. I get the impression that I can only motivate her to cooperate if I know the trigger.

—Consider a new strategy, Ms. Yoshida.

—Okay.

—I mean it.

—I understand.

—And work on your own health values, too. The numbers from the last few days don't look good. You don't sleep enough, you don't move enough, your diet lacks iron. A bad vital score index™ has a direct effect on your performance.

—Yes, I know.

—Do your mindfulness exercises. And get a stationary bike set up in front of your monitor so that you meet your exercise minimum.

—Okay.

—I want to see more progress. Force Karnovsky to cooperate.

—Okay.

—Come back in two days.

—Okay.

—See you then, Ms. Yoshida.

—See you then.

When I get back to the office, my heart rate is at eighty-seven.

I often advise my clients to look at images that they associate with feelings of security to calm themselves in stressful situations. In the browser search field, I type: *quiet space, meditation images, introspection.* The pictures that come up seem generic and redundant to me. Without thinking, I type *happy family* and click on a photo that shows a boy, about twelve years old, sitting on a couch between two adults and laughing. He has something androgynous about him. His smooth dark skin and his fine facial features. An image search leads me to a blog, familymatters.org. I save the image in my private folder and click through the blog entries.

Most of the posts are video files, mainly static shots, showing a biofamily in their apartment. Eating, cooking, cleaning, talking. The image I saved seems to be a thumbnail from one of these videos. The boy in the picture has been running the blog for eight years. His username is Zarnee. His facetag is linked with the name Zarnee Kröger in the persons database. According to his date of birth, he must have just turned seventeen. The timestamp on the photo is from three years ago. That means he was fourteen in the photo, not twelve.

Over the past year, Zarnee has gotten in front of the camera more and more often to share his thoughts and answer questions from fans. He's particularly received a lot of likes for videos with the hashtag *familyblast*—short descriptions of everyday family life and throwbacks with memories of early childhood. I find thousands of reposts, links, and reviews on social media sites and blogs.

Zarnee's profile in the persons database lists his employer as the Family Services Agency™. I know about agencies like that from my studies. You can simulate life in a biofamily by hiring children from birth to eighteen years old and romantic partners for specific periods of time. In training, we studied the use of these and similar services as indicators of mental instability. They fall within a subculture that is generally handled in the literature under the label *nostalgia trends*, or colloquially referred to as *nostalgia porn*.

Zarnee's blog also exhibits clear characteristics of a

nostalgia aesthetic. The videos were either recorded using obsolete devices or the image quality was reduced with filters after filming. Even the embedded closed-caption subtitles have errors, as if they had been created with very outdated software.

Zarnee has been working in the children's division of Family Services™ for eight years and running his blog for the same amount of time. He's among the most highly requested field agents on staff.

Zarnee's blog has grown steadily over the years. I'm surprised that I've never heard of him before. Almost one year ago to the day, he reached the level of having a super-following.

My emotional reaction to the blog worries me. Even though I know it's nostalgia porn, the videos fill me with a strange sense of calm. There's no denying that my heart rate is slowing down. I can't bring myself to close the page for several minutes. I click my way through the image and text files before finally closing the browser app. Then I delete the saved photo and my user data from the log.

Media Usage Log Archive No.: Bc4
Employee: @PsySolutions_ID5215d (Hitomi Yoshida)
Content: familymatters.org
Media Type: Blog
Security Category: Safe
Usage History Data: First access

Closed Caption Track: "A Normal Morning.srt"
so you probably want to know what a normal day looks like in the life of a biofamily ill start with the morning so my bio-mother comes to my bunk in the morning and wakes me up

with a song she sings every morning until i wake up sometimes i pretend i'm still asleep so that she sings longer my
mother doesnt have a particularly good voice and at the
singing castings she was always the first one to get cut but i
still like it when she sings for me its such a nice feeling she
always sings the same old folk song from her child hood anyway then we all have breakfast together with my biofather
my biomother and my biosister and me morning is the only
time when our unit gets sun light thats why we all like the
morning most of all we all like to sit as long as we can at the
breakfast table and dont want to get up at all

9

The Academy for High-Rise Diving™ is located in the second district in the city center. The city planners color coded the steel beams along the facades of the flagship buildings of the twenty inner districts. An effort to give the exteriors an air of relevance and rank that would match the buildings' elaborate interior designs.

From the street, you can't see what lies within the walls of the academy. Likewise, you can't see the trainings taking place above the pentagonal inner courtyard, which lies at the center of the five surrounding main buildings. Dom Wu is the company figurehead. His portrait is displayed in all the entrance halls. The photo, taken in front of the green screen in Aston's studio, shows Wu with a commanding expression, holding up a trophy from the High-Rise Diver World Championships™. Aston has edited Riva into the image, all the way in the background, falling, an unidentifiable human form between the building facades.

Dom Wu's office is located in the penthouse in building 3 and extends over the entire floor. A huge bright hall with just a few pieces of furniture, windows on all sides. It overlooks the entire training area and offers a view that reaches all the way to the outskirts of the city on all sides. Up there, he resembles an air traffic controller, directing movements in the sky, any distraction potentially leading to unthinkable consequences.

Riva and Wu sit opposite each other near the window in two of the chairs designated for meetings, which are arranged in a circle around a glass cube that functions as both a monitor and a table.

Riva went. She responded to my summons. Masters has marked the action yellow with the tracking tool. If the meeting goes well, I can expect green. I was able to follow Riva's commute using PsySolutions' Skycam access. A bird's-eye view of every step from the building to the taxi, the taxi ride along the quickest possible route, and then running from the taxi into the building to get away from the VJs who were waiting for her with their cameras in front of the entrance.

Wu watches the bodies falling past his window, counting seconds. His index finger raps on the arm of his chair. Riva turns away from the athletes, looks around the room.

—How are you, Riva?

—I came by taxi. It's waiting downstairs.

—I'll order you one later when you want to go.

—How long do I have to stay?

—As long as you want. Nobody is forcing you to be here.

Riva laughs and turns towards Dom to look him straight in the eye.

—You had me summoned. If I didn't come, I'd have to pay a fine.

Wu is not an openly emotional man. In the media, he's known for his stony demeanor, not revealing any emotion, regardless of if he wins or loses. Even now, he expresses nothing, no frustration, no surprise.

—Valentina won PanAsia, he says.

Riva is silent. She has turned her face and body away from Dom again.

—She was good, he says.

I imagine how Wu sees Riva now, looking away, defiant. Maybe he remembers Riva as a child, fresh from the peripheries. How she made mistakes in training, resisted his instruction, got angry.

—She wasn't as good as you, he says.

—I'm not coming back, Dom.

—Okay.

—Can I go now?

—You'll lose your privileges, your apartment, Aston, everything. It happens faster than you think.

In the briefing, I advised Wu to approach Riva with a combination of understanding and authority. She needs to be made aware of the breadth of her decision, I said to Wu. The impending consequences. And she must know that you're the only one who can prevent it. That you're on her side.

Riva gets up, not hastily, but determined. She stretches her hand out over the glass cube towards Wu. He takes it, clasping it with both hands.

Riva turns her body towards the door, takes a small step. She's stuck. Wu has wrapped his right hand tightly around her wrist, his facial expression still indiscernible.

—Dom.

—Riva.

—Let go of me.

—Think it over, Riva.

She jerks her hand out of his grip, but he's already let go, making her lose her balance for a moment.

When she gets to the door, she turns around again. She seems to reflect for a moment, and then says:

—I thought of our museum visits the other day, do

you remember? How you would sometimes take the girls with the best scores to the museum.

Dom nods.

I note *Karnovsky mentions museum visit* in my research column. Then I dictate a message to my assistant: *Please find out which museums Riva visited during her time at the academy and if there are any reports about it.*

—Do you still do that with the girls, those Sunday excursions? Riva asks.

She's facing him again, her posture suggests a sudden openness.

Dom Wu shakes his head.

—Do you still remember when we were in the museum with that sculpture, the naked woman, and I couldn't stop crying?

—Yes, Dom says, I remember.

My assistant sends me several files, including a weekly report from the academy's archives. A text passage is marked yellow: *Riva has been noticeably guarded ever since the incident at the museum over the weekend. She only replies to my questions with cryptic answers. I made an appointment for her with Psychological Oversight. Her scores don't seem to be affected.*

—How old was I? asks Riva.

—I don't know, maybe fourteen.

Please try to find video footage of the mentioned incident from the museum, I dictate.

—I think about it a lot lately.

—Why?

—I didn't understand it myself. The crying, I mean. I just couldn't help it. It was as if I had no control over my body. And you never asked me why.

The video that my assistant sends is from an exhibition space in the modern art museum, a spacious hall with various art objects along the walls, particularly photographs. In the middle of the hall there's a silicone sculpture: *Recumbent Woman on Mattress™*.

—You thought she was real, Dom says. You got scared because you thought it was a real woman lying naked on the floor. It was uncomfortable for you. You were ashamed.

In the overhead shot from the surveillance camera, the statue really is indistinguishable from a living human. She's lying on her side and appears to be sleeping on a mattress that is about three feet wide. One leg is pulled up against her body. You can see her pubic hair. Her skin appears slightly grayish or dirty. Pale. Her body looks shapeless, her body mass index much too high. In places where her flesh rests particularly firmly against the mattress, her obese body spreads as if it were melting away.

—I wasn't ashamed, Riva says. It wasn't that. I finally understand that now. I understand a lot lately.

Riva enters the hall at 11:54 a.m. She's dressed up for the excursion, wearing a tight blue dress with a white hem. Her hair is braided into two plaits and pinned up into a bun.

She stops short just past the entrance, as if someone had pressed a button that was connected to her legs. The visitors behind her have to slow down and walk around her. Riva's posture is rigid and tense. Her eyes are frozen on the naked body in the middle of the room.

—Then explain it to me, Riva, Dom says.

His voice sounds gentler than before, fatherly.

—It reminded me of the peripheries, Riva says. Her obesity, her dirty exposed skin, her whole unpleasant presence. There's no one like that in the city. The last time I saw a person like that was in the peripheries. My home.

In the video, Riva starts crying. Her face remains

expressionless, her mouth slightly open, none of her facial muscles are tense. The tears run down her cheeks. She's frozen on the spot, petrified, while the other visitors stream around her like a river with an obstacle in its path. She looks so lost, as if she should be somewhere else entirely. I breathe a sigh of relief when Dom enters the hall, sees her, puts his arm around her shoulder, and then walks over to the statue with her.

—Your home, Riva?

Dom's voice has gotten harder again.

—This is your home. The peripheries were never your home. You always wanted to leave there, you were happy when you finally made it.

—That's true, Riva says.

In the video, you see Dom talking her down, taking her hand and carefully placing it on the woman's skin. Riva, hesitant at first, then repeatedly strokes the surface, as if to verify the reality of the situation. In the wide-angle shot, the woman on the floor looks so real that it's unpleasant to watch the girl touch her naked skin over and over again. Even though I know that it's cold silicone and that it's an inanimate object, I think I can see the skin move from a distance, flinch. I can't shake the idea that the body is soft to the touch and as tender as dough.

—It must have been a subconscious longing, Riva says, that I didn't understand myself. Mourning a loss I hadn't even registered. But it was still in my body. Inside my body.

Her posture has relaxed. She is still standing in the doorway, but no longer in a flight position; instead, she's upright, determined.

—Is that the problem, Riva? That you suddenly long for the peripheries? Then go there for a few days. Find out what it feels like.

Riva shakes her head and smiles.

—No, she says, that's not the problem. I have no problem. You're the one with the problem, Dom. I used to want to jump and now I don't. I used to want glamour and credits and fame, now I don't. And you can't accept that.

It takes a while until Riva calms down in the museum. She and Dom stand in front of the naked body for a long time until she's ready to go. Dom finally guides her out of the hall like a blind woman, his left arm firmly around her shoulders.

—You've been good to me, Dom, Riva says. You used to somehow understand me.

—Then why did you stop?

—Why do you keep going?

Riva's taxi is waiting at the main entrance. She gets in without looking around.

By the time the vehicle merges with the steady flow of traffic, the society blogs are already full of posts about Riva's appearance at the academy. A surveillance video from Dom's office was leaked under the headline *Romantic Strife?* The soundtrack is so noisy that it's almost impossible to understand anything from their conversation—a popular strategy employed by vjs when the actual dialogue in a papavid™ offers too little potential for scandal.

Another blog article is titled *On Parole from House Arrest? The Shocking Details of How Riva Karnovsky is Being Held Hostage in Her Own Apartment.*

Dom calls me immediately after Riva has left his office.

—I didn't get through to her, he says.

—She showed up, she got involved in a conversation, that's real progress.

My voice automatically falls into a therapy tone. Understanding, supporting.

—What do we do now?

—Write to her. Tell her it was nice to see her. Tell her that she should get in touch with me.

—Okay.

—You did well, Dom.

—It hurts me to see her like that, you know. All those years of training. It's such a waste.

—Yes, I agree, I say, and wish he could see my face in that moment, my real sympathy.

I suddenly feel very close to Dom. I watch him as he says goodbye into his tablet and then ends our call.

My head hurts. I take two pills and close my eyes for a minute. Then my tablet vibrates with a new message. It must be Royce Hung, finally getting in touch.

The message isn't from Royce, but was sent automatically from the server operating system. Hugo M. Masters tagged my log from the meeting between Riva and Wu as *To be revised.*

I sign into my profile at the partnering agency. Royce Hung hasn't rated our date. Maybe I should write my review first. Maybe he's trying to be polite by waiting. I start filling out the form. Five stars seems too enthusiastic to me, he could interpret that as too eager. I decide on four stars first, but click on five shortly before sending. Anything else would be rude.

I find it difficult to shake the image of the naked woman in the museum. Her morbidly obese body. It makes me think of my first visit to the peripheries, my first compulsory casting. After customs, there was another world awaiting us behind the wall. We pressed our faces against the bus window and pointed to the poor, dusty streets, the gray block buildings. Within minutes our bus was surrounded by people waving to us. Adults and children in an uncontrolled mob. Sticky people, making faces and stuffing bad, unhealthy food into their mouths. One woman caught my eye in particular. I'd never seen such a fat person before. The jumper she was wearing didn't cover her entire body, flesh pushed its way out in rolls on all sides. I felt sick. While the others on the bus laughed and pointed at the people, I turned away from the window and looked down until we had to get out.

10

After seeing Riva exhibit more readiness to communicate with Dom, I hoped to take advantage of it by asking Aston to organize a telephone coaching session. After making contact, he holds the tablet out to Riva.

—Riva, I say, trying to sound as open and caring as possible, can you hear me?

Riva doesn't answer. She's sitting on the sofa and her eyes are fixed on the opposite wall, as if she were deciphering an invisible message.

—Riva, you don't know me. I understand that this is strange. But sometimes it can be helpful to talk to someone who's completely disconnected from your life. I just want to talk to you. Person to person. I want to understand. Can you help me understand you?

Aston holds the tablet so that the round speaker opening is turned directly towards Riva. He's standing next to the sofa. His posture suggests uncertainty. I advised him not to sit right next to Riva or put the device down because then she could turn it off.

—Imagine what it must be like for Dom, I say. He's lost a close confidante, a colleague, a daughter of sorts. And he doesn't understand why. We don't want to force you into anything, that's not what this is about, Riva. But at least give us the chance to understand why you broke your contract. Not me, forget me, you don't know me. But

Aston. Dom. Your colleagues. They don't deserve to be left in the dark, helpless. Your fans.

Riva lets out a laugh, the first indication that she's been listening.

—You don't think your fans deserve to understand why you left? Why not, Riva?

Riva doesn't answer. Her facial expression is stony. Her eyes stay frozen on the opposite wall. She didn't even look at Aston when he came into the living room from the studio and started the audio connection.

—Imagine what it would be like for you if one day Aston just suddenly started walking on his hands. That's all he did, all day and all night. Wouldn't you like to know why? And in your case, Riva, it's a much more extreme situation because he sees, because everyone sees, everyone who cares about you, that you're not well. And everyone is worried about you, Riva. Everyone wants to help you. But you have to tell us what happened. We want you to get better. Don't you want that too?

The corners of Riva's mouth move, her lower lip quivers. She looks at Aston, his arm has begun to tremble slightly from holding up the tablet to her. Riva's gaze is cool, almost condescending. Aston looks back at her, unsure, and then takes a step towards her. With a quick hand movement, she knocks the device out of his hand. It crashes onto the floor with a bang and lands with the screen facing down. Aston backs away.

—Riva? I call out and hear my muffled voice echo in her apartment.

Riva leans over the edge of the sofa.

—Riva, I can understand your anger, I say. I want—

Before I can say anything else, she's already broken the connection. She leans back on the sofa, no emotion can be read from her facial expressions.

Aston shakes his head, shrugs, and then goes into his studio. The door loudly clicks shut. Riva doesn't move.

Unsuccessful results, writes Masters in the log file.

The color marking the action does not change.

At least she had an emotional reaction, I want to write back. But I don't want to appear unreasonable.

In order to escape my disappointment, I search the web for distractions. After several news portals, I suddenly find myself back on familymatters.org.

Media Usage Log Archive No.: Bc8
Employee: @PsySolutions_ID5215d (Hitomi Yoshida)
Content: familymatters.org
Media Type: Blog
Security Category: Safe
Usage History Data: Frequency of use low, average once per day.

Closed Caption Track: "Presents.srt"
my biofather always buys us presents when he has enough credits like yesterday when he gave me this clown that you can wind up and then he laughs and shakes his head just like this hahaha my biosister got scared and cried my father always brings her sweets because its the only thing she likes then she stuffs them into her mouth all at once so that her hole face is full of chocolate i tried to play with her with my clown but she just cried she said that she wants a dog so my father will probably bring a dog with him next time he actually does every thing we want because he loves us so much

11

Riva has used her tablet three times in the last twenty-four hours. A breakthrough. According to her media usage log, she searched the internet for images using the keyword *peripheries* and downloaded certain ones. Generic photographs of streets and houses, typical concrete blocks. But also several individual portraits of children playing outdoors. One of the pictures was taken at night. It shows a girl, about three years old, with a circle of light around her. The visual effect doesn't seem like it was added later, but instead was created naturally by the girl spinning in a circle with burning torches in her hands. I couldn't find any connection between the people in the pictures and Riva through facial recognition.

While checking the tablet, the data analyst made a discovery. The installation history shows that a diary application was deleted shortly before Riva broke her contract. The analyst promised to recover the account as quickly as possible. Since the app operates with multiple encryptions, it may take a few days. At least there's hope of gaining direct insight into Riva's inner state. Even Masters reacted enthusiastically to the news.

Still, I'm running out of time. Masters has been putting more pressure on me every day. In the online tracking tool, he's marked all of the ongoing actions orange or even red, and project progress is displayed as insufficient. I have to get her much closer to the intended state by the next investor meeting. Because of my bad review, I didn't get a performance fee and I'm afraid I won't have enough credits for my rent next month.

My order log for Call-a-Coach™ has been empty for two days. I wonder if I lost my account without having been informed. It's probably just a coincidence. Despite the lack of nightly interruptions, my sleep is getting even worse. The sleep-summary graph on my activity tracker shows restless periods. They occurred at regular intervals when I reached for my tablet, half asleep, to check if I missed any calls.

Everyday needs cost too much time. Since my contract requires a minimum level of physical and mental fitness, I can't cut back on my already neglected mindfulness and fitness exercises anymore. I've limited my sleep time to five hours and got a warning from my tracker in response, which Masters marked red in the daily report. I asked him if I could do the video analysis from home for a while in order to waste less time traveling between home and work. Masters has approved this for the time being. My argument that I needed a geographical change for new stimuli made sense to him.

From the corner of my eye, I noticed how he was rapidly taking notes as I left his office. I suspect that it was a performance report. Judging by his stern expression, I'm going to have to expect a warning.

Masters's demeanor brings back the memory of my last encounter with my biofather. It took place in a similar-sized office with a similar air of authority. I was four years and seventy-seven days old. One of the caregivers had unexpectedly taken me out of the morning program and brought me to the director's office. I was wearing the institute's play uniform. The girl's version was a blue knee-length dress made of water-repellent stretch fabric. The institute logo was printed on it in white—the silhouette of a dog's head in a circle. The logo is firmly embedded in my memory. It was printed on everything we owned. I liked the idea of a dog; it's cold, wet snout and thick, warm fur. More than that, I liked the associations with trust and reliability. Dogs seemed like the perfect companions to me and I dreamed of owning one as an adult, not realizing that it was incompatible with a successful workday.

I was led to the management office, a part of the institute that I'd never seen before. The first things I noticed were its expansive size and the window wall; backlit in front of it, the two men standing at the desk looked like silhouettes. My caregiver greeted them both with a brief handshake and left the room. From close up, I first recognized the institute director, who came around every Monday to visit the classes. And then I noticed the other man—my biological father. I'm not sure anymore how I knew it was him, the caregiver probably told me. From the institute's archival data, I know that he and my bio-mother came to the institute together in the first year of my stay, but I don't remember it. After that, the frequency of his visits dwindled more and more.

When I was two and three years old, he sometimes came for meetings at which, according to the minutes, I wasn't present. At the age of four I only saw him this one time in the director's office. The reason for the appointment is noted in the minutes as a *finance meeting*. My father wanted to exempt himself of any payment obligations and remove his name from the contract because he and my mother had ended their relationship.

He looked down at me and put his hand on my head. It's the only time I can remember my father touching me.

His hand felt heavy and warm. At first I wanted to brush it off, but then I started to like it. It gave me a sense of security, similar to how I felt when I was restrained on one of the daybeds at the institute. They would strap us to them when we got in trouble. Other children would squirm in their beds for thirty minutes and try to free themselves from the restraints. But I usually accepted my situation after just a few minutes and would submit to it entirely. Once I had accepted it, my inescapable position suddenly turned into a space of happiness. I would close my eyes and breathe into the bed, which seemed to engulf me like a hug. The feeling that I could do nothing and that nothing was expected of me other than to breathe in and out. I relaxed every muscle of my body, so that the straps would only lay loosely on me, and often didn't even notice that a supervisor had already released the fastener. In a whitepaper from the childcare institute on the benefits of physical restraints in child rearing, I once proudly read a case description on my own positive reaction to the bed.

My father left his hand on my head while he talked to me, making it difficult for me to see his face with his arm blocking my field of vision. In the meeting minutes, there are no pauses or verbal fillers. His fluid manner of speaking suggests that he had prepared his remarks in advance. Because I've read the report several times since then, it's difficult for me to distinguish what I remember from what I read. In any case, I think I remember that I perceived the meeting as loving and positive and that the reason for parting ways was clear to me, but didn't frighten me. To me, my biofather was an unknown, but friendly man who was in some way connected to me. And now he was calmly explaining to me that we would not meet again. I recall his forearm, its thin curly brown hair, and the vague smell of a popular deodorant that I had recognized from other men his age. There was something familiar and at the same time foreign about him. He was like the men who would show up in our classrooms from time to time, talk to one child or another, and then disappear again.

When my biofather had finished talking, the caregiver stepped back into the room and led me out. From the corner of my eye, I saw my father turn to the head of the institute and exchange a few words with him; his face was filled with disappointment and anger, which seemed to contradict the previous interaction. I couldn't forget that face for a long time, and later came to the conclusion that my biofather had been dissatisfied with my behavior towards him. He had probably expected a livelier, more active child, someone upset about his departure, crying, or even reaching for a hug.

Seeing a similar expression on Masters's face when I left his office yesterday brought back the self-disappointment I had felt after meeting my father. Just as I read over the minutes from the conversation at the institute, I tried to remember every detail of my reactions during the meeting with Masters in order to evaluate my misconduct. I've come to the conclusion that Masters interprets my request to telecommute as a withdrawal and admission of failure, maybe even as a surrender.

12

It's as if all of my communication channels are having a software malfunction at the same time. The data analyst hasn't decrypted the diary application yet. Within a short time, the frequency of incoming messages has been cut in half. In the last four days, I've only had one single Call-a-Coach™ request, which was handled within five minutes. Most of the time, my tablet is silent. I even get fewer advertising messages.

Royce still hasn't posted a rating yet, either. His last login is indicated as today's date, 9:50 a.m.

I click my way through his profile in search of any clues I might have missed. Something showing that I was wrong about him. Showing that we're not a good match. All of the information is still the same. His values largely correspond to my values. Nothing deviates from the memory I have of him.

I write him a short note via the agency's messaging service: *Royce, how about a second round? Let me know.*

I delete the text from the message field without pressing enter. Then I type it again, word for word. I add an *if you have time* and delete it again. Then I delete *let me know.*

Royce, how about a second round? My finger lingers just above the return key.

I've made a list of possible reasons why he hasn't

contacted me yet: He hasn't seen my review. He's too busy. Something happened, an illness or an emergency at work.

Up to now, I've always been able to assess interpersonal communication with a certain level of accuracy. I've never found myself clinging to any misguided notions about whether someone would or wouldn't contact me after a date. I was sure that Royce would get in touch. I'm sure that Royce will get in touch. He just needs a reminder.

Royce, I had fun the other night. How about a second round?

After sending the message, I click the refresh button a few times to see if he's read it yet. No green checkmark appears. Maybe it's an application error. Maybe he wrote to me long ago and the message didn't get through.

I check the spam folder. Empty.

I hit refresh. The page comes up again, unchanged. I enter Royce Hung's name into the search fields for medical facilities. No results. I write him another message: *I hope everything's okay?*

He doesn't respond. The time and date of his last login are still the same. I reload the page again and again. Log out, in, out, in.

In the evening, still no answer. I can't stand being in front of the monitor anymore and wind up outside on the street. I haven't just gone for a walk like this in years. It feels strange. My steps get faster and faster as if someone else were controlling my legs. I must look like I'm rushing to an important business meeting. The rhythmic sound of my steps on the asphalt.

As teenagers, Andorra and I would sometimes get restless and go outside, aimlessly walking around without knowing where we wanted to go. I listen to my steps, close my eyes for a few seconds, go blind. Then I tear them open, afraid of colliding with something or someone, or walking off the sidewalk and into the road. There are hardly any pedestrians, but an incredible number of cars. Rush hour. I imagine the people sitting inside behind their windshields, staring at the rear lights of the car in front of them.

A man comes towards me. His pace is as fast as mine. We race past each other. Then I'm seized by the thought that it could've been Royce Hung. I turn around and see his silhouette shrinking in the distance.

I have to stop thinking about him.

The city smells like machines. All industrial buildings are located outside of the city in the peripheries. Maybe it's an illusion, my nose is no longer used to the outside air and is misinterpreting it.

The smell of the peripheries always made me nauseous as a child. I would already start to feel sick days before a compulsory casting. During the castings, I had to take medication to avoid vomiting on stage. The heat, the smog. My skin grayish, sickly after just a few hours. I showered several times a day. Andorra made fun of me. She didn't mind the dirt and the bad air. She was excited when the next casting approached. She believed in being chosen, in making the early breakthrough. I reminded her of the statistics and that we weren't dependent on being chosen. That our education at the institute separated us from the unpredictability of a casting jury. But Andorra lost any semblance of being a rational person when it came to our future. When I had long since given up on the dream of high-rise diving, she forced me to continue training with her for the castings. For a while, our morning trainings started so early that we could hardly sit up by the time we got to breakfast.

All of a sudden, I'm standing in front of a bar. Based on the logo, it's part of a cheap chain. I look in through the window. The interior is the same as in all of their other locations: an oval bar with bar stools in the middle, upholstered seating areas along the walls. It's decorated in the retro-trash™ style with red walls, golden candlesticks, and baroque mirrors interspersed with flat screens.

It's been about ten years since I've been to such a place. As teenagers, Andorra and I sometimes ended up in a bar on our nightly excursions.

I'm overcome with a feeling of shame. I don't want to remember it. But I go in and sit at the bar anyway. The seating niches are occupied by people with low to middle pay grades. They're here on the break between their day and night jobs. Their ties loosened, blazers on the coat racks.

One woman stands out. She's sitting in a corner niche with four men. The men are all wearing similar run-of-the-mill business suits, maybe even the same brand. The woman, in contrast, is wearing a striking evening gown made of a shimmery fabric. Her hair is pinned up in a complicated hairstyle. Her long earrings turn in the flickering light of the screens. From time to time she laughs, her eyes wander through the room and stop on one of the screens. A short papavid™ is being played on the news. It shows it-girl Roma waving from a hotel window. The caption announces that her health has gotten worse. There are also clips of fans placing candles and flowers in front of the hotel and holding banners up to the window: *We love you. Get well soon.* According to the documents in the data archive, Aston has been commissioned for an editorial with Roma. He's hardly spent any time in his apartment in the last few days.

I order a flydive™. Then I remember that it's Riva's signature drink. I change my order to a vodka martini. The bartender shrugs and pours out the tonic that was already in the glass.

Masters will reproach me for drinking alcohol without any social obligation. I think about just not putting it in my nutritional profile, but then decide against it. I tell myself what I tell my clients: once you start with self-deception, it's hard to stop. That's what the logs are for: to capture moments you're not proud of. That's the only way you can confront it and do it differently next time, better.

I swig the alcohol like juice, feel it enter my bloodstream, relax my body. It takes away the unpleasant feeling that has settled in me. Soon I will have access to Riva's diary and solve the mystery of why she broke her contract. I will guide her back to the right path.

The woman in the evening dress smiles at me and raises her glass from across the room. I lift my glass, notice that it's empty, and order another.

She comes over, sits next to me.

—Boys club, she says with a nod towards the sitting area in the corner.

I take my martini from the bar, we toast. She's drinking a flydive™. My facial expression must have been too obvious. She looks from her glass to me and back.

—Not a fan of the flydive™?

—No, I am, I say. Just a few bad associations. The woman nods to me, almost conspiratorially.

—I can imagine.

—No, no. I didn't mean it that way.

—No, me neither, the woman laughs.

I wish she would go back to the corner.

I feel a dragging pain around my temple.

I take my tablet out of my pocket and open my pain log, enter the time and type of headache. The woman stays in her seat, catches a glimpse of my display, nods understandingly.

—I also have problems with chronic headaches, she says.

I empty my glass in one go. My throat burns, I am warm.

—I have to go, I say.

—But you only just got here.

—Back to work, I say.

—What do you do?

—Accountant.

Keeping with its retro style, the bar has no pay-point™. You have to pay the bartender. I want to ask for the bill, but the bartender has disappeared behind the counter.

—Are you worried about Roma, too? the woman asks.

I turn away, look around the room for the bartender.

—He'll be back soon, the woman says, as if he'd told her personally.

I sit down again.

The woman looks at me, awaiting a reply.

—Do you have other plans? I ask, looking at her dress.

She shakes her head.

—Last night I dreamed that Roma died, she says. I couldn't get myself to calm down for hours. Do you know that kind of dream? It seems so real that you can't shake the feeling, even after you wake up? As if the dream were stuck to your body?

Andorra often had dreams like that. In my memory, I'm wrapped around her, embracing as much of her body as I can. She's curled up like a hedgehog, but her back is soft. She needs someone to hold her, to whisper to her so quietly that she can only hear it when their mouth is right against her ear: Everything's gonna be okay™, everything's gonna be okay™. My breath disturbs the fuzz on her earlobes, she presses her ears against my lips like feelers. She was crying in her sleep, wailing, the nightmare is still in her body. Everything's gonna be okay™, I whisper and systematically stroke her like a cat from head to tail. Andorra presses herself into my hand and it's almost as if my hand weren't resting on the fabric of her institute nightgown, but directly on her skin, which is damp and cold from sweat.

Andorra's nightmare periods sometimes lasted several weeks. Her cries always woke me up before her. Sleep seemed to be a natural state for Andorra. I envied her for it. She didn't have to worry about it in the evening like I did. As soon as she closed her eyes, she drifted off. The nightmares seemed to me like a fair price to pay. It was only when she lay in my arms, exhausted by the horror that her own mind had conjured, when I could feel her fear in my body, that I felt ashamed of the thought. I tried hard to make up for the betrayal, to release her from the clutches of her nightly terrors. When Andorra's breath got quiet and steady again, becoming almost inaudible, I would allow myself to close my eyes and hope that my consciousness would soon be carried away, too.

The bartender appears from a door I hadn't noticed before. He greets the woman next to me and pours her a new drink.

—She wants to pay, she says, looking at me.

The bartender holds the device out to me, I press my tablet against it.

—Nice to meet you.

The woman holds out her hand and I shake it briefly.

—Feel better! I hope your headache improves.

I thank her and quickly walk out of the bar. In the door,

I turn around again and see that the woman is already engrossed in conversation with the barkeeper. When she notices that I'm looking at her, she turns to me and waves.

When I get back to my apartment, Riva's in bed. Motionless. I listen closely to the audio from the bed camera to make sure she's breathing. Aston is in the studio preparing for his job tomorrow.

When I activate my Call-a-Coach™ profile, I already have two requests. I breathe a sigh of relief. The inactive period seems to be over. I let my finger hover over the callback button on the touch screen, but can't get myself to click on it. Instead, I open the partnering agency app and check Royce Hung's profile. No activity. Only the last messages I sent, unread: *Royce, I had fun the other day. How about a second round?*

I lean back and close my eyes. According to my employment contract, I have to respond to therapy requests within half an hour of being called. One of the clients added a short text describing his problem. The subject heading is: *Fear of termination*, and then: *I made a big mistake.*

The other caller didn't specify a subject, only a category: *sexuality*. I click the callback button. The man answers on the first ring.

—Thank you for calling me back.

His voice profile identifies him as Zeus Schmidt, freelance data analyst. What if it's actually Royce Hung, I suddenly think. It could very well be that he gave me a fake name. Many users take an alias for their public dating profiles and don't reveal their identity until they're sure of the relationship. I've always had problems distinguishing people by their voices. Maybe because I focus on so many other aspects when I talk to people. And the individual character of someone's voice seems the least important.

—How can I help you? I ask, and then, following the inquiry procedure guidelines: Please state your full name, your department, and your position.

I confirm the data stored in the language and identity profile on the server.

—It's a private problem, the man says, not a business problem in the strict sense.

—That makes no difference. This service covers all kinds of problems.

I hear a sound created by a jerking movement, the friction from his face rubbing against on the microphone: the man is nodding.

In general, my clients prefer to use headsets for their consultations rather than the speaker function. Even if they're alone in the room, it gives them a heightened sense of privacy, an atmosphere of trust.

—What's it about? I ask.

I'm also wearing a headset, as it allows me to move freely during consultations without impairing the quality of the conversation. I walk slowly around the room, first to the window, then to the kitchen. I run my left fingers across the furniture.

—I've got something going on with a woman who's not sterilized.

I make a sound to confirm that I'm listening and that he should continue talking. It also suggests that I've heard about this type of thing many times before. That it's a known problem and can therefore be overcome.

—And now I can't get it up.

—Understandable, I say. That's a very natural reaction.

Again I hear the sound of the microphone brushing against his skin, I imagine the man sitting upright in an office chair and nodding.

—Have you had a vasectomy?

—Yes, but sometimes that doesn't work.

I sit down on one of the bar stools at the kitchen counter and nod, just as I imagine the man on the other end of the line is doing.

—I'm nodding, I say.

—What?

—I'm nodding.

—What does that mean?

—I agree with what you're saying.

—Okay.

—Because you can't hear me nod, I told you.

—Okay.

—Or can you hear it?

The man is silent, I only hear his breath.

—I heard you nodding a few times before, that's all.

I've never made such meaningless statements during a consultation before. I've abandoned the procedural model entirely. I'm already going over the conversation he's going to have with the Call-a-Coach™ human resources representative in my head. He'll probably schedule it by tomorrow morning at the latest, if not tonight, depending on how many overtime hours he works.

—It's strange, I say, when you have as many non-visual consultations as I do. You start to hear certain gestures, purely physical gestures, you know?

I hear the man nodding.

—Once, I say, I had this client, one of your colleagues, maybe even someone from your department. I think he may have satisfied himself during a consultation.

I hear how the man's breathing changes, how he holds his breath for a moment.

—I'm not sure, I say, if he was aware that I could hear

his movements. His manner of speaking had hardly changed. He must have done it many times before, he was almost completely in control.

I imagine the man getting up from his office chair, stunned, and now wondering whether he should inform the complaints office or pull down his pants.

—We talked about very mundane things, he was nervous about an important presentation; he'd been promised a promotion if everything went well at the conference. And he just took it out in the middle of the conversation and masturbated. You might be wondering, how can I be sure, but I can interpret the sounds on a call really well after so many years of experience. You collect new information with each conversation, which then creates connections in the brain and refines certain skills over time.

I hear no movement on the current call anymore.

—I didn't hear him ejaculate, either he waited until the conversation was over or he was extremely controlled ...

—Listen, the man says. If I were you, I would delete this conversation recording from the log.

—Which do you think it was?

—I'm hanging up now and we're going to pretend we never spoke, okay?

I nod instead of saying anything. I nod until the man has ended the conversation.

Then I delete the callback from the log and the archive data, I delete the cache and the hidden file elements. I can't stop nodding until I'm in the shower with hot water running over my body, burning against my skin.

The half-hour callback period for the second client has already elapsed. I consider calling him anyway, but an overwhelming tiredness takes hold of me and I barely make it to bed, naked, my skin red and hot. In the morning I don't wake up until the alarm goes off for the third time, even though I can't remember hitting snooze twice.

13

Masters has summoned me for an unscheduled performance review. This type of invitation is always paired with the anxiety that your supervisor intends to criticize your work, but now I'm afraid he wants to fire me.

When I arrived at the PsySolutions building, I ducked into a corner in the green room to take a breath before entering the lion's den.

Please come to my office as soon as you get here. HMM.

The message appears on my tablet just as I'm about to sit down on one of the waiting-room chairs.

—Fuck, I say almost aloud into the empty room and immediately regret it.

I feel the throbbing of an oncoming cluster headache. Despite my interest in the psychosomatic, I'm annoyed by my body's psychosensitivity. I stick to what I advise my clients to do. I breathe deeply. In a calming tone, I say to myself: Your emotion doesn't belong here. Your emotion comes from the past.

Are you here? HMM.

The notification sound reverberates in my skull. In the hallway, I make sure that the security camera can't record any change in my gait. No emotional disturbance.

My knocking sounds as it should: firm and short.

Masters is sitting cross-legged on the floor of his empty office. It's gotten even more austere since my last visit. There's not even a desk. Just the floor-to-ceiling windows and the potted plant standing in front of them, as if it were enjoying the view.

—Good morning.

—You asked me to come by?

Trained ears would be able to hear the tension in my voice, the overstretched vocal chords, the higher pitch than usual. I hope that Masters, as always, is too busy with more important things to be listening that closely.

—Sit down.

Masters gestures to the floor in front of him. My body awkwardly moves towards him, knees first. The fatigue suddenly makes me weak. My back curves in a way that must make me look like a human ball on the camera. I try to straighten my back. My eyes land on the door behind me, it's open. I jump up.

—Leave it, leave it. I just need to fire you real quick, then you're right back out.

My heart is pounding. Masters must have heard about my Call-a-Coach™ conversation. The client must have filed a complaint against me. My activity tracker starts beeping because my heart rate is too high. I can feel my heart beating in my throat. I try to breathe calmly, just as I advise my patients to do in such moments. Breathe away the panic. My body is frozen.

Masters laughs.

—Ms. Yoshida, how long have we known each other now?

—Just about four months.

—Then you should know by now: I'm kidding. I'm kidding. Relax. I'm just kidding.

My heart beats a little slower. I hear the blood rushing to my ears. I barely manage to slide down onto the floor without lying down entirely. Just stretched out on the ground like that.

—I read your failure list, Masters says. You hit the nail on the head with a lot of things.

My heart starts racing again.

Inconclusive results.

No improvement of overall condition. Conflict intensifying.

Complete refusal to cooperate on the part of the subject.

Under the file name *Failures*, I created a spreadsheet listing all possible criticisms of my work. The document was for self-monitoring purposes, so that I could work to improve any issues. The items fill two pages, neatly written one after the other. I should've remembered that Masters also has access to my private folder on the server.

I try to nod to show that I am listening and contemplative. I'm suddenly filled with the fear that my nodding will drag me off course again like it did the night before. That I could say something I don't want to say. I bite my teeth firmly together. As a child, I was so afraid of saying something inappropriate that my jaw muscles were regularly sore.

—You still don't have a clear diagnosis, Masters says.

—No.

I close my mouth immediately after speaking, my teeth resolutely pressed together. I stop nodding.

—And your interventions have been unsuccessful, Masters says. The subject doesn't read your messages. She doesn't talk to you.

—She went to see Dom Wu, I say. That was a step in the right direction.

—Not much came of it, Masters says. You have to push harder, Ms. Yoshida.

—I'm on it, I say. According to the legal department, we can start with harsher penalties tomorrow.

—Then start immediately.

I nod.

—The data analyst is collecting more childhood data, I say. There are still some inconsistencies.

—What do you want with childhood?

Masters shakes his head and then turns to the window, away from me.

—A first trigger, a traumatic experience.

—Stick to the methods of modern psychology, Ms. Yoshida! Don't waste your resources. Childhood is over, childhood is irrelevant. You know the studies. Riva Karnovsky grew up in the peripheries. Everyone grew up in the peripheries. So, that alone has no influence. It's better that you concentrate on solving the problem. The implementation of therapeutic interventions.

—I think that the measures will be more successful if they're based on the findings of the situation analysis.

—According to the timeline, the situation analysis should be done already. Investors expect results. Measurable changes. I can't go to the steering committee meeting with the current implementation status.

I nod and keep clenching my teeth together. Masters looks at me. I sense that he's noticed the tension in my jaw muscles. I relax my mouth and smile.

—We need a plan of action, Ms. Yoshida. Riva Karnovsky is a tough nut to crack, so you'll have to use stronger equipment. We need your creativity. You were recommended to me as someone who's creative. Think of something. If the woman doesn't cooperate with you, then maybe she'll cooperate with someone else, if you know what I mean.

—Yes.

—Are you also still working for Call-a-Coach™?

—Only on call at night.

—That's too much, Ms. Yoshida. A project this important requires your full attention. You can't give one hundred percent with a second job. But we hired you one hundred percent, didn't we?

I nod and try to relax my facial muscles while pressing my lips together.

—I can't forbid you from doing that job, Ms. Yoshida. But, from what I've seen, I can tell that you have too much on your plate.

Again I wonder if Masters listened to my botched consultation. In the interview he praised my telephone counseling work in particular. How can I make him understand that I can't give up Call-a-Coach™ because I need the credits? That my living space is actually too expensive for my income level and that even a single lost client can mean relocation.

I look over at the potted plant. A drop of water drips from a leaf and onto the smooth flooring beneath it. He must have watered it just before I got here.

As far as I know, building regulations forbid real plants in the offices.

—Do you understand me? Masters asks.

—Loud and clear, Mr. Masters.

Masters smiles and leans back.

—You see? Now calm down, stretch your legs. Peace is paramount. Why do you think I'm doing this digital cleanse? My mindfulness scale is almost at one hundred percent.

—Congratulations.

—So, listen, think of something radical! I'd like to present a completely new strategy at the investor meeting. Got it?

—Got it.

—Send me a proposal by tomorrow. Then we can discuss the details.

—Okay.

I push myself off the floor and shake my supervisor's hand.

—Firm handshake, Masters says. I love it. That's why I hired you.

When I get to my apartment, I don't see Riva on the split screen. I zoom in on every corner of the room and finally find her behind the couch, flat on the floor, staring at the ceiling. Sometimes it feels like she knows she's being watched. As if she's intentionally hiding from me in the moments when I'm not paying attention.

I create a new file: *Action plan*. But I can't concentrate.

I click around on Zarnee's blog. It's the only thing that significantly lowers my heart rate. It's more effective than any mindfulness exercise. I hate that I can't resist the content, even though the posts disgust me. On *Casting Queens*™, I always hated the segments where the presenters visited candidates in their run-down apartments or approached them on the street. It made me queasy whenever they left the clean stage area. Andorra, on the other hand, was always fascinated by the peripheries.

—In the peripheries it gets so hot sometimes that people aren't allowed to go outside for days, she once said. You can't even imagine.

We sat under the UV screens on the institute roof and drank our vitamin drinks.

—How do you know? I asked.

—I was there.

—We were there together, I said, we're there together every year and it's never been that hot.

—You were never really outside, you were only in the casting parlors.

—You never went outside either.

—You weren't there that time.

I knew Andorra was lying. It would be impossible to get past the security checks and cross the border without a permit or registered escort.

Andorra lied a lot, she thought that lies made life more exciting. That it didn't count as a lie if you only changed a few details and basically agreed with what was being said.

—You went to the peripheries without me? I asked her.

—Yeah. One time when you were taking the aptitude test all day. I got myself an excursion pass and went.

—Why didn't you tell me about it?

She shrugged and tilted her head. She looked me right in the eye in a way that only she did. Then she pressed her index finger to my lips.

—You would have blabbed, she said.

The view from the institute's roof terrace was not very good. The building was smaller than the ones around it. Sometimes we looked for our reflections in the glass walls that towered in front of us.

—But what if I blab now? I asked her. Andorra slowly ran her finger over my lips.

—You have very soft lips.

I snapped at her finger and held it between my teeth. Andorra screamed and I let go. I left small dents in her skin.

—You were never in the peripheries, I said.

Media Usage Log Archive No.: Bc11
Employee: @PsySolutions_ID5215d (Hitomi Yoshida)
Content: familymatters.org
Media Type: Blog
Security Category: Safe
Usage History Data: Frequency of use medium, average
three times per day.

Closed Caption Track: "Hugs.srt"
most of you probably cant imagine what its like to live with
your biomother you see the pictures but you cant really
under stand the feeling my biomother is always there and
she always comes and hugs us she has such a warm soft
round body like a protective shield that raps around you so
that nothing can happen to you as a child she always carried
me when i was still a very little baby she never put me down
even when she went to the bath room now of course im too
heavy for that but she still hugs me every day and gives me
kisses and says that shes proud of me and all those things

14

Roma is sitting in the back of a dusky hotel room. The only daylight shines in through a tall window to her right, the rest are covered. It highlights her distinct profile even more. The chin, the lips, the nose, the forehead—all well-known from the media. Roma is positioned in such a way that every journalist who enters the hotel room immediately sees how beautiful she is, objectively beautiful.

The Romacam™ website allows you to select different rooms at the press hotel. The choice of camera perspectives is limited. This is how they avoid diminishing the value of the professional visual materials.

Roma's assistants move around her like waves on a predetermined course. I click my way through the rooms until I find Aston. He's sitting in a waiting room with other vjs, journalists, and photographers. When his name is called, an assistant has him put his fingerprint on the touch screen under the release agreement before bringing him into the room.

—Sit in the armchair opposite her. Don't go any closer than that chair. You can move around the room to take pictures, but you can't get any closer.

Aston nods and walks slowly towards Roma. His gait becomes more formal on its own, official. Roma takes advantage of the ten-minute break that she has scheduled between each press date. She holds her tablet as close to her ear as possible, presumably so that her fans can't hear the messages that the tablet's audio assistant is reading to her. One of her personal assistants bends over as close to her as possible without touching her. Rumor has it that a single touch could cost Roma her life. The assistant announces the new guest. Aston smiles when Roma looks over at him. She smiles back.

—Just photos? Roma asks as Aston sits down in the designated chair.

—Just photos.

She nods and straightens up a little in the armchair, takes on a more intentional posture.

—You may begin, one of the assistants says, suddenly standing behind him.

Aston lifts his camera up to eye level. I imagine how Roma looks in the same position, but framed by his viewfinder. Clearer. How the frame accentuates the shape of her body. Emphasizing beauty. Creating meaning. He clicks the shutter release again and again, changing his position in his armchair, possibly uncertain of whether he should leave that spot.

—Should I do anything differently? Roma asks.

It seems to me like she is asking because she feels his hesitation and wants to make him more comfortable. She presents herself from all sides, turns her profile towards him, faces him directly, then looks past him, down, up, right into the camera.

You can't see her illness. Not from the security camera's perspective. I expected her skin to be translucent, shimmering. I imagined her like a doll, exactly how she looks in the thousands of professional photos, exactly how she'll look in the dozens of photos that Aston is supposed to add to the collection.

Maybe it's the lighting, the room is too dark, the only source of light is the afternoon sun from the one uncovered window.

—It doesn't show at all, Aston suddenly says. Roma freezes in motion.

The words have barely escaped his lips when he presses them tightly together again, as if to prevent another outburst. You can see the horror on Aston's face; everyone knows not to mention her illness.

People immediately start posting on the Romacam™ website at a rate of multiple comments per second. *Did you hear that?—What the fuck?—That guy is the worst.—Doesn't he have any manners?—Who the hell is this clown?—Aston Lieberman, that photographer who was dating Riva Karnovsky.—Is dating.—I heard they broke up.—Didn't he kidnap her?*

You can't really see the look on Roma's face.

I imagine her pupils completely dilated. Her face full of contempt.

—Sorry, Aston says.

The assistants are all standing at attention, ready to grab Aston by the arm and drag him out of the room. Their eyes are on Roma, the person behind the wheel.

—I know, Roma says. You don't see it so much here, it depends on the lighting. I prefer it that way, in the dark.

Aston begins to take photographs again in order to conceal the explosive nature of the moment. A violation of the rules of interaction can mean a professional ban.

—The shimmer is added in the post-production, Roma says.

—You can find the terms for the post-production in your release contract, says a voice from the group of assistants, who seem to have relaxed again.

—I think you're even prettier like this, Aston says.

Roma laughs using her bashful schoolgirlgiggle™.

Aston dares to get up and leave his chair. He walks around her, maintaining the specified distance.

When he leaves, she waves from her seat and winks at him.

—You can be glad that we aren't reporting you to the press authorities, an assistant says as the hotel-room door clicks shut behind him. Luckily for you, Roma didn't take it personally. Others would not be so accommodating.

Aston apologizes several times, squeezes her hand.

—All right, she says almost sympathetically. You got away with it this time.

As he rides down in the elevator, I enter Roma's name into the search field and look at hundreds of images of her body. *Corpo vitreous* is among the keyword tags, *glass body, Roma, star, fragile, deadly disease.* You can also find the release contract for her photos. The tools for creating the shimmer effect, the ordered sequence of editing steps, the color and light values, brush strength, and degree of transparency are all listed in detail. Unedited images are destroyed by a data cleaning service. I suddenly wonder whether they just invented the disease. Whether this is all just a gigantic advertising campaign.

The thought of touching her to see if she breaks pops into my head. The image of a body shattering, bloody fragments on the hotel carpet.

You should've touched Roma, I write to Aston via our encrypted communication channel without thinking.

From the security camera in the hotel elevator, I watch as he reads the message, shakes his head, and then puts the tablet in his pocket. His facial expression indicates disapproval. He looks around the elevator and crosses his arms in front of his chest. His reaction is perfectly understandable. He must think I'm tactless and incompetent. Why would I write that to him?

Aston, I type to correct my absurd impulse, *Riva needs your help.*

He pulls the tablet out again, reads my message, puts it back in his pocket.

She desperately needs medication.

This time, he holds the device in his hand a little longer before letting it disappear into his pocket. He hesitates.

You can see for yourself how thin she's gotten. That she's not sleeping properly. That her fitness values have rapidly deteriorated.

I think I can make out a hint of concern in his facial expression.

You're the only one who has access to Riva. The only one she trusts.

I see him shaking his head slowly from left to right.

Aston, she needs medication. To help her mood.

Her motivation. Her appetite. Her sleep.

The elevator arrives at the lobby, but Aston doesn't move. The doors close again. Aston holds the tablet's microphone up to his lips and dictates an answer: *No.*

If she continues this way, she'll die, I write.

He stands in the elevator, the doors open and close again because no floor has been selected. His expression becomes more introspective. He moves his knees as if he were walking in place.

How do you imagine that happening? I hear him dictate quietly, the message appears almost simultaneously.

I'll send you a prescription and then you mix the medicine into Riva's drink. Ideally in water, so you can add ice cubes. A man enters the elevator and presses a button to go to a different floor. Aston pushes past the man to get out. He leaves the hotel, taking short quick steps until he's out of range of the security cameras.

Okay, his message appears a few seconds later on my tablet. *I'll try.*

15

—Is it my fault? Aston asks.

Partner exhibits feelings of guilt, I note. Riva doesn't respond. She's sitting cross-legged at the window and watching traffic.

—At least tell me what I did wrong, Riva, and I'll make it up to you. If you don't go at some point, they'll take away our housing privileges.

—Fine with me. I'll live somewhere else.

—We have a credit union, Riva. My credits are your credits. If you go down, I go down.

—The credit union was your idea, Riva says.

Aston grabs his hair and pulls at it so hard that individual strands come loose. He bends down to Riva and holds the hair up to her face.

She starts to laugh. She lifts her head and looks him straight in the eye for the first time today. As far as I can remember, it may even be the first time since the project started. *Eye contact,* I note.

Aston opens his fist, lets his hair drop on the floor in front of Riva, and leaves. He slams the studio door so hard behind him that one of the photo frames comes loose and falls to the ground. Riva stares at the frame. She fixates on it for nearly a full minute with an emotionless expression on her face. Then she jumps up.

Within fractions of a second she's already on the other

side of the room. She lunges at the frame and kicks it with full force. It slams against the wall. A crack forms across the display surface and the head in the image is split in two. It's a photo from *Dancer_of_the_Sky*™.

Riva grabs the partition wall closest to her and throws it to the ground with all her might. Frames slide across the designer floor. The second partition clatters against the wall, a loud crash suggests that there's more damage that isn't visible. One wall falls after the other, shards fly through the room.

I don't see Aston come in. He's suddenly there, amidst the chaos, screaming her name, but she isn't listening. She smashes his digiframes with a systematic determination that reminds me of her training videos. Aston doesn't try to stop her, just stands there and watches, as I sit here and do the same.

Riva lets go of the display panels, throws herself on the floor, drags her fingernails hard across the surface until she starts bleeding. She doesn't make a sound, but her face is twisted with rage. The teeth clenched together, the corners of her mouth pulled back. Her skirt is torn and has slipped upwards, so that it barely covers her thighs. The blouse that was previously tucked into the skirt is hanging out in some places.

Aston watches her as if he's lost all connection to himself. And even when he finally embraces her and pulls her close, his eyes look past her at the fallen furniture, the shards, the trails of blood. Riva squirms out of his grip, lets herself fall, just lies there. I zoom in until I can see only Aston, his stiff, empty expression, eyes frozen somewhere on the opposite wall. I can see the tears welling up in both of his lower eyelids and then streaming down his face at the same time. My hand intuitively moves towards the monitor. I pull it back and dictate a message: *We have to adjust the medication.*

At first he doesn't react to the vibrating notification on his tablet, but he eventually pulls it out.

Riva looks almost as if she's asleep on the floor.

No, writes Aston. *I won't go along with it anymore. I won't give her anything else.*

I send him links to studies that prove the effectiveness of the drugs. I highlight the sections that talk about the initial period of time required until the medication starts to take effect.

No, Aston writes.

Then he drops his tablet on the floor next to Riva and leaves.

At night, Riva appears before me as a grunting creature. I open my eyes and see her crawling on the ground a few steps away from me. She rears up like an animal, pants, claws at the vinyl flooring in my apartment until her fingernails come off and bones emerge.

I wake up, I'm hyperventilating, my body is engulfed in fear. I find the light switch, but even the warm orange-yellow glow of my bedside lamp does little to calm my pulse. I count seconds, slowing each breath down until time and space have normalized. Until I know where I am and what happened.

The sheer force of the strange rage sticks to me like sweat. It feels as if it's aimed directly at me, as if I alone am its target, Hitomi behind the monitor. And then I recognize the feeling.

Riva's rage is Andorra's rage. She hits the wall with her fist and the dull sound reverberates throughout my body. Riva's fingers are curled into Andorra's fist, pounding against the bedroom wall at the institute. Riva's lips, pressed tightly together, are Andorra's mouth. Torn open, screaming shit, shit, shit, saliva dripping out, mixing with tears and snot. Her fist hitting the wall until the skin on her knuckles tears and tiny droplets of blood are left behind on the plaster. Until she sinks into her bed and buries herself under the blanket and everything is quiet. How often I saw Andorra so beside herself in the months before her disappearance, sudden attacks of uncontrollable furor. And how I felt responsible, begged her to stop.

Andorra's numbers on the adaptation scale were always lower than mine. In the end, though, they even dropped below the minimum values. During our weekly efficiency reviews, she regularly received penalty points and additional assignments. She was threatened with expulsion, and I was afraid that it wasn't just an empty threat, as Andorra claimed. High adaptability is essential to success in life, as we were told time and again.

I remember how Andorra laughed and then shrugged

—What can I do? she said. I am what I am. Our trainers saw it differently. Among the institute's core convictions was that personality was changeable. You just had to work on yourself hard enough. As Andorra's adaptation values got worse, mine steadily got better. On my final diploma, I had achieved the highest marks in my class.

16

Riva's diary app has been decrypted. The data analyst uploaded a total of two hundred and seventy-nine text files, all of which were written by Riva. His research shows that she had everything deleted shortly before her breach of contract.

The entries are from the last five years. The usage chart shows phases in which Riva wrote down thoughts and experiences daily, sometimes even several times a day, then times when she didn't compose a single entry for months.

The analysis provides new psychometric data. Riva's psychograph has changed considerably over the last two years, contradicting the analysis of the media data in many respects. Maybe the downside to her extensive media coaching is that Riva has managed to manipulate her public image over a period of time.

In the first three years of app usage, Riva's entries correspond to the image that she presented to the outside world. But then it changes drastically, the texts become note-like, fragmented, and inaccessible. Riva appears less balanced, more irascible, less goal-oriented. Her willingness to perform, her self-discipline, and her enthusiasm for competition diminish. Instead of descriptions of her progress during training, she started creating more and more numbered lists of what are presumed to be memories with no apparent purpose.

Archive No.: LK1514_a-l
File Type: SuperSecretOnlineDiary™
User: @GoKarnovsky (Riva Karnovsky)
Relevant sampling of keywords: *neuroticism—motivational deficit—aggression—frustration—fear—pessimism—passivity—diminished ability to cope with stress—limited willingness to perform—psychosomatic symptoms—nostalgia*

Sample_ jk6h1
Blue silver. Like the sea of metal. Like the flickering of the shooting star online, 17 CP, but it's worth it, it's really worth it. Blue silver and not aqua orange. The investor wants the blue silver suit. The investor WANTS the BLUE SILVER suit. The investor is angry because I'm wearing the wrong suit at media training. 250 CP penalty. Dom's face is red. Can't you read.

Sample_ jk6h2
Diligence and care. Diligence and care. Diligence and care. Diligence and care. Diligence and care. Diligence and care.

Sample_ jk6h3
1. The plant arms in the concrete. The house is gray. Greenish gray or bluish gray. A rectangular box with rectangular black windows. Plants grow into the house from below. They come out of the windows or grow in from outside.
2. The girl. The girl is spinning in a circle. It's completely dark. The girl is holding sparklers and spinning, she doesn't stop spinning. A sister? Probably not. Where did she come from and where is she now?
3. The wall. It's dirty and sticky. Someone cleaned it in some spots and painted little people with blue and green paint. If I take several steps back and stretch my neck, I can

see a narrow strip of city behind it. The tops of the highest skyscrapers, their lit-up windows. The city lies behind the fog. It lights up the fog from the inside. It looks blurry, hazy.
4. The woman. I can't see her face. She's holding her arm over her eyes because she's looking at the sun. In the background, the block of gray houses with black windows. The woman is strong, she stands tall.
5. Burning skin. Heat and dust. Breathing is difficult, as if there isn't enough air in the air.

Sample_ jk6h4
Avoid the following topics: politics, religion, sexuality. Avoid personal opinions, jokes, rumors. Avoid sharp edges. Avoid direct sunlight. Avoid the feeling of hopelessness. Avoid the outer districts. Avoid touching unwashed hands. Avoid make-up brands if you don't have a marketing contract from them. Avoid squinting or opening your eyes too wide. Avoid the signature triple turn in bad wind conditions. Avoid overestimating yourself, otherwise you're worm food, otherwise they'll have to scrape you off the ground.

Sample_ jk6h5
Penalty for violation of team spirit, soon I'll be out of credits. You're a role model, damn it. I laughed, I don't know why, I felt so helpless. Stella got a warning for violating the hygiene rules because she didn't change her tampon for over four hours.

Sample_ jk6h6
1. The stage in the peripheries. Stairs that you have to climb. Starting numbers, my name written on lists. (Does that mean I could already read then?)
2. A person whispering in my ear: Try hard. Do your best. This is your chance. The rest of the person is no longer

there, her face, her hands. Only her voice.
3. Stumbling and catching myself. Hot blood shooting
into my head. I stumble and I smile, I don't lower my head.
I catch myself, just as I learned.

Sample_ jk6h7
The girl with the short-shaven hair screams: You're famous!
Fresh from the peripheries, shaved for transport. Happiness
in her eyes. I see her spot me and then scream. You're
famous! I give her an autograph card. She bobs up and
down. When I walk over, her outpouring of joy surrounds
her like a puddle.

Sample_ jk6h8
I can't get rid of the image, lava hitting the ground. We
had post-fatality training and got blockers. But I can't stop
thinking about her. The wind was actually good. Dom thinks
she did a sloppy job packing. There's a rumor that it was a
technical failure. The new model malfunctioning. I wonder
what she was thinking when she realized she wouldn't make
it. Whether she was disappointed in herself.

Sample_ jk6h9
Like my blood caught fire and is burning me from the inside
out. Dom always tells everyone that I never get sick. I told
him: Dom, I'm sorry, I'm sick now. Really.

Sample_ jk6h10
1. Dom, picking me up from the transport and leading me
through the academy. He says: This is your new home. Are
you happy? I'm completely intoxicated.
2. Dom's office before the morning training, and I say: Do
you remember when I arrived and you picked me up? And he
nods and smiles, and suddenly everything is good between
us again.

Sample_ jk6h11

I can't find the off switch. The only time there isn't any noise is when jumping, total silence, only the gray-blue of the sky and the city below me.

Sample_ jk6h12

1. A woman dancing, two kids. On the street, in the spray of a sprinkler. The wet fabric against her massive body. A bent little finger. Her mouth open. Water on her lower lip. The asymmetry of the laughing face. A child reaches out to her, she picks him up and whirls him around in a circle.
2. Round holes in the smog, the sunlight piercing through. Cones of light, falling like searchlights on dry land. That's why everything is black, only those spots are chosen by the light.
3. The sound of rain. Open roads. Landslides. Rain that never stops. Drumming on the roof. I fell asleep in the rain, under the rain. When I lie in bed now and can't sleep, I long for that sound. Maybe I should download one of those audio files that simulate nature sounds, so I can fall asleep.

17

—I don't agree with your diagnosis, Masters says.

I try to cover up my insecurity by straightening a crease in my blouse. After the successful diary analysis, I was expecting praise and extra credits.

—You mean the analysis of the diary data? That's not a diagnosis per se.

—The investors will understand your report as a diagnosis. Dom Wu has made explicit statements about which terms should not be used in the reports in order to prevent any legal claims against the academy on the basis of damages. Burnout is on the blacklist.

Masters's potted plant has disappeared. There's now a small golden Buddha statue in its place. In front of it, there are several small bowls with offerings and incense sticks that haven't been lit.

—Those were the findings from the psychometric data analysis, I say.

—Change them.

—I don't understand what the findings have to do with Dom Wu.

—Ms. Yoshida, burnout is not a valid diagnosis. Ms. Karnovsky has completed various happiness and resilience trainings as part of her training program, far more than those recommended by the health authorities. The academy implements a rigorous mindfulness program. Riva Karnovsky has always received high resilience scores on her aptitude tests. Your diagnosis is obsolete and plain illogical, Ms. Yoshida. Riva Karnovsky is only twenty-four years old. That would be like diagnosing yourself with burnout. Fresh out of training. Not a year on the job market yet.

During our studies, we learned to lead resilience trainings. Our clients, managers like Masters himself, would move through the room on one leg and balance pencils on their heads. To understand what it's like to be insecure. To lose balance, control. They took the exercises seriously, just as they took all professional challenges seriously. After the pencil had fallen, they would become even more focused. But it was clear to all of us that the exercise must have seemed absurd to them. None of the men and women we trained could imagine a real loss of balance. In fact, it was particularly challenging for us to imagine, too. We had all worked too hard on our stability for that.

—To be honest, the findings also surprised me. Maybe the data should be checked again.

Masters's facial expression changes immediately. I take a deep breath. I don't want to drop any lower in the employee ranking. I focus my eyes on the Buddha statue to center myself.

—Maybe the emphasis could be shifted to a nostalgic episode, I say. Karnovsky mentions childhood memories again and again in her diary entries. It could be explained by an age-related hormonal change that caused a temporary personality disorder.

Masters nods in agreement.

—Okay, he says. That sounds good. What interventions do you derive from it?

—We need to gain more direct access to the subject, I say. We need a person on site. Someone she's willing to work with.

Masters looks at me like he's waiting for something. It makes me feel insecure for a moment.

—I have a field agent in mind, I say. Could be perfect for the job. It's a somewhat unconventional idea.

—Ah?

I hesitate before I explain my plans to him, trying to emphasize the firmness in my voice. From time to time he nods, but his expression remains critical.

It's strange how often being in Masters's office makes me think of the management office at the childcare institute. Of my biofather. As far as I can remember, my father had nothing in common with Masters. He was a tall man with dark eyes who expressed himself in quiet, thoughtful movements. Not like Masters, who, despite his strict mindfulness program, always seems jittery, bobbing up and down on his toes during meetings and constantly moving around through space. What connects them, I realize, is not their similarity, but my reaction to them. Like my father, Masters makes me feel as if I've already disappointed him when I enter his office. A feeling of a fundamental inadequacy that can never be improved.

18

The boy looks exactly like his headshots. Slender and youthful. Tender brown skin. His facial features are soft and changeable. With the right clothing you could turn him into practically anyone. A twelve-year-old girl. An adult businessman, a flight attendant, a dancer. At Family Services™ he's employed in the ten-to-eighteen age category.

I know him as Zarnee. He has many screen names. Many messaging accounts. And the blog.

He moves fluidly, as if there were no air resistance and no gravity. He had started practicing ballet as a very young child and then one day he suddenly got bored. In his blog he describes the multi-year episode with a nonchalance that one would consider implausible, if there weren't such an air of authenticity to each of his words. Nothing seems made up. Watching his video postings is like having a private conversation with him, huddled together and in hushed tones. Eye to eye.

As a child, he trained for a year from morning till night and then performed very well in the castings. It wouldn't have taken much more. But he suddenly changed his mind, decided to stay in the peripheries, started blogging. For a while, he prepared himself for the science castings, studied mathematics and physics on his own. But he also eventually got bored of that. He passed a series of exams, was transferred to the A-level castings. Even achieved a life-changing-moment™. But he didn't accept the invitation; he forfeited his place at the academy.

He has been working for Family Services™ for eight years. According to his credit score, his income should have long been sufficient to move into an apartment in the city. His order history at Family Services™ includes a total of five hundred and seventeen assignments.

When I see him approaching on the security camera at the building entrance, I immediately know that I made the right decision. It's raining, the temporary parking area is disgusting and gray. The delivery drivers are indistinguishable in their raincoats, quickly scurrying from their cars to the entrance. He's the only one walking slowly and leisurely. Without an umbrella or coat. As if he were taking an afternoon stroll in one of the city parks.

When I shake his rain-soaked hand, the clamminess lingers for a while.

He sits down in my chair without it being offered. We're in the same therapy room where I met Aston. It's just a coincidence that this specific space was free.

I sit opposite him in the client seat. Masters will reprimand me for it later, but I'm not that worried about the distribution of seats at this point—now that I've finally found a promising intervention that can produce significant results.

—I'm only doing it because it's so absurd, Zarnee says. It's the first time I've received a request and had to read it twice because I was so surprised.

—I'm happy to hear it.

—Otherwise, I'm not a fan of the city, he says. You read my blog. I've already gotten plenty of better-paying offers.

This is the only thing I've seriously considered.

I nod and let him talk. He gives the impression of wanting to get some things off his chest.

—I know Riva, he says. I followed her early career. She's something special. She's creative. She's not one of those divers who only perfects the standard forms. They only perform what was given to them. No matter how well you do a thing, if you're just performing someone else's ideas, it's pointless. Perfectionism is not a compliment. No one wants to admit it, but it's true. What counts is creation.

He looks at me as if his criticism is in reference to me personally. His eyes are forceful. I'm not used to looking someone straight in the eye without a monitor anymore.

—We have different motives, he says, but we want the same thing. I want to live in a world where there are only divers like Riva, and you want her to fulfill her sponsorship contracts. We won't meet in the middle, I don't give a shit about your contracts. But I'll help you anyway, because I want to meet Riva. Because I want to see her dive off a skyscraper again and do her thing. In any case, she shouldn't sit around in her apartment like a caged animal. We have so little time, don't you think? We should use it to live.

I nod and smile. I lean back. He starts talking again. There's something almost manic about him that's contagious. I feel more awake than before.

—I have no ethical concerns, he says, as if he were answering a question. You don't get far by following rules, either legal or moral. I know you disagree with me, that you would even say the opposite, but I don't care. It's not about educating the people around me, you know. The world can't be saved. But individual people can. You can still coax them out of their misery and "revive" them, as you so nicely put it.

—Coax them out of their misery, I say. Also an interesting formulation. I could use that for my investor's report.

—Please don't, he says, then it would lose all meaning.

I laugh to mask a hint of annoyance. His expression tells me that he noticed it anyway. He hasn't taken his eyes off me since the moment he entered the room.

—What I'm trying to say is, he continues, you have your reasons and I have mine, but we agree. I'll sign your contract and you don't interfere. Leave me to it. I know what your goal is, and I'll stick to it. You can rely on me.

He holds out his hand.

I shake it briefly and then give him the tablet with the terms of the contract, showing him where to put his fingerprint and where to sign.

—Would you like to read it again?

—No.

—The intervention has been legally approved. You will move in within the next few days.

He gets up and heads towards the door without shaking my hand again.

—Your blog, I say, once he's almost completely disappeared behind the door.

—Yes?

—Did it all really happen that way?

—Does it matter?

—It creates a feeling, I say, of authenticity.

The boy nods and closes the door behind him.

I watch him walk out of the building on the security cameras. He's walking just like before, strolling leisurely like a dancer. When he crosses the parking lot to leave, it has already stopped raining, but the changing weather appears to have no effect on his demeanor. At one point, he jumps over a puddle that has formed in the middle of an empty spot. I write a message on the custodial forum about the irregularity in the pavement. I mark the location on a screenshot of the parking lot. He's still visible at the edge of the picture, a slender figure without a jacket.

19

Riva enters the administration building at 8:23 a.m. *Hesitant steps*, I note, and in the comment column: *Uncertainty, worry.*

I almost want to reach out across the countless streets and houses that lie between us and give her an encouraging nudge. Speed up the process.

Yesterday, Aston begged Riva not to agree to the reduction of housing privileges, to appeal. At least to buy a little time until they can come up with an alternative, a solution.

—What would that be? she asked, without sarcasm, but rather exhaustion. An alternative?

—I have a new assignment, Aston said. Roma for Celeblife.corp. The deadline is next week. My agency hopes to get a lot from it. I could get a higher VIP status.

He took her laughter personally, stormed out of the room, and didn't show his face again until the next morning.

There aren't many people in the halls at the administration building. Riva checks the building plan, takes an elevator. She makes her way through the building and has to backtrack a little at one point. She missed a turn somewhere. She doesn't seem to notice that she's quietly saying the room number aloud to herself like a mantra. 1222B, 1222B, 1222B. She appears distant, distracted.

Inside the room, Riva sits in the designated chair. She looks into the camera in front of her. Her expression is different from the expression I see on the hidden cameras in her apartment, which occurs unconsciously, by chance. Here, her eyes are piercing, they cut into me. Riva stares at me as if she knew who was sitting at the monitor. Despite the hint of defiance in her eyes, the insecurity is still clearly visible. I wonder if the situation reminds her of her first interviews, from before she learned to hide any discomfort.

One of the officials from the reassignment office starts the program from his workplace four districts away.

—Please provide your full name and identification number.

—Riva Zofia Karnovsky, MIT 2303 1151 8600.

The computer-generated voice is gender-neutral to prevent legal complaints.

—You have a full understanding of why we summoned you?

—Yes.

—Would you like to appeal?

—No.

—In that case, do you formally agree to the reduction of your housing privileges due to non-performance?

—Yes.

—This applies to your accommodation in district 2B, building 7662, apartment 14C, which you currently share with Aston Lieberman, identification number KLT 2307 4423 0010, correct?

—Yes.

Answers clear and fast, response time less than 150 milliseconds, I type. *Karnovsky wants to get the session over with quickly.*

I'm happy to see that Riva's behavior is in line with my

prognoses and that she isn't showing any resistance. My intervention is based on Riva's readiness to adapt.

Initiation of intervention successful, I note in the daily protocol. I have a good feeling.

—Do you have any other housing privileges?

—No.

Riva's media training at the academy taught her not to give answers like that. The following interview rules are emphasized in the code of conduct: *Never give mono-syllabic responses! Always formulate full sentences, even if the interviewer asks questions that could be answered with yes or no. Every answer must have media value.*

—Would you like to make an official statement?

—No.

My analysis of the online comments showed that the public was not bothered by the mechanical way that Riva gave her answers in the last few interviews before the breach of contract. Only Dom's weekly reports note that he had been urging her to work on her energy in interviews.

—The reassignment proceedings will be initiated in the next few days, the computer speaker says. We'll inform you electronically about the specific terms. Please sign here.

Riva uses the stylus to enter her initials into the blinking field on the monitor and then holds all of her fingers up to her digital fingerprints until a check mark appears.

—We wish you a pleasant day.

After the identity verification, Riva just stays there, sitting in her chair. Her expression seems absent on the camera.

When Riva doesn't move, my pulse starts to rise. Her behavior is absurd. It doesn't seem deliberate to me, but more like a system malfunction.

—Please leave the building via the marked route.

Riva doesn't move. It's as if an all-encompassing fatigue has taken hold of her body. What will happen if she just sits there until the end of the day, blocks the room, disrupts productivity? I'll be held responsible.

I pace back and forth in front of my monitor, counting the seconds. I hope Masters isn't logged in and watching the action live.

—Please leave the building via the marked route.

After exactly thirty-five seconds, Riva stands up, her legs trembling. In the hallway, she heads for the bathrooms and splashes cold water on her face, sits in a stall on a closed toilet cover.

I sink into my office chair, breathe a sigh of relief.

Karnovsky found the appointment strenuous, I write in my report. *Just leaving the apartment requires more energy for her than average. She is no longer accustomed to being in public.*

Good work today, appears on my screen shortly afterwards, *HMM.*

I save the message in my personal archive and lean back. I can't help but smile. Masters's recognition fills me with joy all the way to my fingertips.

I watch Riva as she sits on the toilet seat and breathes slowly and purposefully, in and out, just like she learned in diving training. My breathing automatically conforms to hers.

When she returns to the apartment, Aston is already there waiting for her.

—What did they say? he asks.

He seems nervous. His camera is sitting on the floor next to an armchair instead of hanging around his neck.

—Nothing, Riva says.

She is visibly taken aback by Aston's interest. His eyes

follow her every move as she walks to the kitchen counter and reaches for the shelf. Her quick hand movements, putting ice cubes and gin into a glass.

—You want one, too?

—Riva, what did they say?

—Nothing.

—That can't be. They don't summon you for no reason.

—I had to sign something.

—What?

His facial expression is fearful, almost childlike. Riva doesn't seem to notice his nervousness. She's withdrawn, sipping her drink, slowly walking to the window.

—What did you have to sign?

—Why do you care?

The sentence probably came out more aggressive than Riva had planned.

—Why do I care? We have a credit union, Riva.

—Then dissolve it, Aston.

20

A notification sound pulls me out of my thoughts. Riva hasn't moved much over the past several hours and I keep drifting off during observation. At first, Riva doesn't react to the tone coming from her tablet on the living-room table. It's the default sound for the apartment buzzer. She probably expects Aston to open it from the studio. At the fourth ring, she slowly stands up. Aston left the apartment three hours ago.

When she gets up, her lack of movement over the past few weeks is visible, she rises sluggishly from the floor, needing both hands.

The boy enters the room. He's wearing one of his outfits from Family Services™. A simple T-shirt and jeans. Neutral, in order to avoid overwhelming Riva, as we agreed. He didn't gel his hair the way he usually does it. It's a little curly, a bit messy, but not wild. He looks very young with it styled this way. Riva might assume that he's around fourteen.

—Hey, he says.

His voice is soft, very different from the interview. Kinder.

Riva silently considers him, absently running her hand through her unwashed hair. The boy looks around the room, letting his eyes drift across the reconstructed photo walls, the photographs, one after the other. He takes his time. Looks back and forth between Riva's picture and Riva.

Then he drags a suitcase into the apartment, a huge monstrosity that appears disproportionate next to his slender, boyish body.

He holds his hand out to Riva.

—Zarnee, he says.

—Aston's not in.

Riva's voice sounds raspy and hoarse.

—Okay.

Zarnee lowers his hand. Riva looks past him through the open apartment door and into the corridor.

—Where's my room? Zarnee asks.

—The studio is next door.

—And I sleep in the studio?

—What?

Riva now seems to actually see him for the first time, looks him straight in the eye.

—You want me to move in to the studio? Zarnee asks.

—Aren't you one of Aston's models?

—I'm moving in with you. I was promoted from the peripheries. You agreed to the terms, didn't you?

Riva turns away from him. With her left index finger she draws shapes into the condensation on the outer edge of the drink she's holding.

—Sorry, Zarnee says. I thought you knew. I can come back later, but I still have to report the move in today.

Riva takes a step back to allow him into the apartment. She doesn't look at Zarnee as he enters. Her eyes are lowered, her shoulders hunched forward.

Zarnee walks past her and puts his suitcase in the middle of the room.

—Where should I put my things?

Riva just shrugs and goes to the kitchen. She kneels

down on the floor in front of the counter, runs her hand under it, and pulls out the plastic top that she had been playing with for days at the beginning of the observation. She sits with her back to the counter and spins the top on the floor in front of her.

Regressive behavior, I note. My gut churns with the fear that Masters will end the intervention as soon as it starts.

Zarnee watches Riva attentively. Then he tilts his suitcase to the side and opens it. Riva doesn't react, she is focused on the top. Zarnee digs into his suitcase, unfolded clothes spilling out over the sides, and then pulls something out. A strange object made of various pieces of wood of all different types and sizes, as if it were crudely glued together by a child's hands. My image search for similar objects doesn't yield any results. I send my assistant a close-up screenshot with a request for identification.

Riva keeps spinning her top as if she were alone in the room. When Zarnee goes over to her, she doesn't look up.

He imitates her posture with his legs outstretched to either side so that their feet almost touch. Then he presses on one of the pieces of wood with his thumb. With a crunch, it disappears inside the object and the other elements shift to create a new, more elongated constellation.

Riva looks up. Her top falls to the side. She doesn't pick it up.

Zarnee presses on the wood again, it makes the same noise again, the object changes shape again. It must have some sort of mechanism inside.

My assistant responds to my request, explaining that he could not identify the object.

—What is that? Riva asks.

—See for yourself.

—What's it for?

—It changes its shape. You never know exactly how it's going to come out.

—And what do you do with it?

—You press on it somewhere and it changes.

—No, I mean, what's it for?

—You press on it somewhere and it changes, Zarnee repeats slowly.

They look at each other. Something seems to be happening between them that I can't quite classify. A sort of silent understanding.

Zarnee holds out the object to Riva. She takes it and presses on it. When she hears the crunching sound and the elements shift in her hand, she smiles. I've only seen her smile twice since the beginning of the assignment. I can hardly keep up with my notes on the transformation of her gestures, facial expressions, posture.

—Where did you get it? Riva asks.

Her upper body is leaning forward. She's abandoned all gestures of refusal.

—My biofather made it for me, Zarnee says.

—You know your biofather?

Zarnee nods.

They sit opposite each other on the living-room floor, as if they'd been sitting like that for years, mirroring their postures down to the smallest detail. The effect of the encounter is already undeniable. I can feel my breathing begin to get calmer.

21

Aston is standing in a backstage area at the casting halls. He's deep in conversation with a woman. Without having to change the camera perspective, I can already tell from behind that it's Roma. Her assistants and bodyguards are standing in a cluster around them. Aston laughs and then I hear Roma join in. They give the impression of having a close bond. Breaking news flashes on the *Casting Queens*™ website: Roma is a surprise judge today. The comment area grows every millisecond, overflowing with excited messages from fans in the peripheries who have decided to drive over to the casting halls as fast as they can to at least catch a glimpse of her. Opportunities like this rarely arise for fans whose travel permissions are limited to the peripheries.

The cluster of assistants moves towards the artists' dressing rooms with Roma and Aston in the center, still deeply engrossed in conversation. A vj comes running out of a side entrance and plants himself in front of them. Because of the crew's slow reaction time, he manages to get a clear shot of them together, which turns up shortly afterwards in the news alerts on the most important gossip portals. *Is Riva's Old Lover Roma's New Lover?*

Roma and Aston. That would be a surprising development if it were real. It's been a long time since I've bothered reading the fact-checking websites that verify whether or not certain rumors are true.

I forward the alerts to Zarnee to test how Riva responds to the news. He's sitting next to her on the sofa in the apartment. The leftovers from lunch are on the coffee table in front of them. A domestic scene. As if they had already been living together for a long time.

Riva has begun to eat more regularly since Zarnee moved in. Her vital score index™ seems to rise daily. In the tracking tool, Masters has highlighted these changes positively. My project progress is finally in the green. I've been able to book more than five hundred credits as an achievement bonus. The investors are growing more and more confident. On the second night after Zarnee moved in, I felt so relieved that I almost slept an entire eight hours and, for the first time since the beginning of the project, I got an achievement star in my activity tracker log. Neither Riva nor Andorra appeared in any of my dreams that night. Instead, colorful Escher-style houses, falsely constructed, but still habitable. People whose faces didn't remind me of anyone in particular and who actually smiled as they moved towards me. I woke up with a feeling of lightness and carelessness that I hadn't felt in years.

Zarnee reads the forwarded headlines and, just as I requested, holds out his tablet for Riva to read them.

Riva laughs.

—What's so funny?

—He'll be happy, Riva says.

—Aston?

—That he's finally making headlines without me again. It would be nice for him to find someone with a higher credit score.

—That's cold, girl.

I see Riva's grin freeze. She looks at Zarnee, her head slightly tilted.

—Do you think there's anything to it? she finally asks.

—I don't know. Are you even still together?

Frozen in suspense, I await her answer. Finally Riva is being asked the questions that I've wanted to ask her since the project began. Before Zarnee's assignment, I loaded a list of questions onto his tablet using our protected communication channel. I've been adding to it daily. So far, I haven't been directly involved in his conversations with Riva. He should gain confidence in interacting with her. I want him to feel like he can act autonomously. His own initiative is crucial to the success of the intervention.

—No idea, Riva says.

Both burst out laughing at the same time. They remind me of Andorra and me. At some point, our classmates gave up asking us what was so funny.

—Maybe you should straighten that out, Zarnee says, giggling. Riva shrugs. Riva's one hundred and twenty-fourth shrug, according to my notes. A passive-aggressive gesture that makes the other person feel provoked when repeated.

Zarnee grabs Riva by the shoulders and shakes her.

—What are you doing? Riva says.

—I'm shaking the tension out of your neck.

It's almost uncanny how well the intervention is working. Within a few days, Riva looks like a different person. More relaxed. More open. Almost talkative. Now Zarnee is even leaning against her a little. I highlight it bright yellow. This is the first time since the beginning of the project that Riva has tolerated physical closeness.

—Can I ask you a personal question? Zarnee asks.

Riva nods.

—Why did you stop diving?

The muscles in my neck tighten, I turn up the volume.

I hope Masters is logged into the live feed, so that he witnesses the crucial moment.

Riva turns away from Zarnee and looks out the window.

She shrugs.

—I don't know.

—Of course you know.

—It's hard to explain.

—Try me.

Zarnee doesn't look directly at Riva, but his body is turned towards her. He gives her space, while creating a basic sense of closeness at the same time. His behavior is exemplary. After this project, I should offer him a steady collaboration. Why don't you move in yourself? Masters asked when I presented Zarnee as a candidate.

I don't have the right profile, I replied. And there would be the risk of her finding out who I am.

The truth is that it never occurred to me to go into the field myself. I prefer media-based client conversations via talk, chat, or video app. Direct encounters contain the risk of not being able to control my facial expressions or gestures. I would also prefer to use video chat instead of meeting with Masters in person, but he likes direct communication with his staff. Probably because it gives him a sense of power to summon subordinates into his office.

—It's okay, Zarnee says into Riva's silence, you don't have to.

You're almost there, I write to him, *dig deeper*.

I see Zarnee pick up the tablet and read my message, but he doesn't react.

Instead, he starts checking his blog and dictating short messages to his fans. The response rate on his blog is very high.

For a while, Riva sits silently next to him and watches.

—Doesn't it bother you? she then asks.

She bends over to look at his display. Their cheeks almost touch.

—What?

—Answering all those stupid questions. Always the same questions, all day long.

—For stupid questions, there are stupid answers, Zarnee says.

Riva looks at him and grins. Her face has changed since Zarnee's arrival. It's less stiff, more elastic. I make a note of it and see that Masters is logged into my document. I wonder if he's really reading the logs or just checking on my efficiency. My focus when developing an intervention. The constant notifications I receive about Masters's document changes and updates in the tracking tool make my heart rate rise to unhealthy levels and my tracker starts beeping. From time to time I temporarily mute the notification windows at moments like this, even though it's not permitted by my contract.

Pound five three seven, but that only applies to Fridays, Zarnee says into his tablet.

Riva leans against him, watches his fingers move across the touch screen, her eyes wander along his thin, boyish arm. Suddenly, she pushes up his T-shirt sleeve.

—What's that?

She runs her index finger over a bulge on the inside of his upper arm, just under his armpit. I can't really zoom in to see because Riva's hand is blocking it. It could be a subdermal implant.

—That depends on who you ask, Zarnee says.

His expression is impossible to read, but seems to be enough for Riva. She doesn't ask any more questions, just concentrates on the bulge, the long, narrow foreign object under his skin. Zarnee continues typing, undisturbed by the interruption, dictating blog commentary into his tablet.

—My favorite animal, he says, what a creative question! My favorite animal today is the water bear, tardigrade, master of false death.

22

Over a hundred notifications appear on my screen at once. News alerts for Aston Lieberman. An accident occurred while shooting *Casting Queens™*. Aston himself doesn't appear to have been hurt. Most of the news articles contain the same video footage from the live feed on the *Casting Queens™* website: a raw recording from the filming of a recurring segment called *Discoveries* in which a VIP spends several days in the peripheries as a talent scout. It's not a conventional casting, but instead the VIP surprises talented children while they train. The host sneaks from gym to gym, to sports fields or classrooms. Particularly popular are the street scoutings, where candidates are selected for modeling and acting careers. Anyone who's chosen gets an LCM™ and is accepted directly into a city academy or talent agency without any further casting requirements. After three months, the VIP then visits her protégés on site and decides whether they're allowed to stay or are sent back to the peripheries.

In this video, the VIP is Roma. Aston is there with his camera to accompany her.

—And where are we going now, Roma? you can hear Aston ask from off-camera.

Conversations with the VJs or other crew members are edited out for the official broadcast, but they are also the exact reason why the live feed has so many subscribers.

—I'd say it's about time to head to a high-rise diving™ practice site, don't you think? A little birdie told me that there are some great talents near here.

Roma winks in the direction of Aston's camera.

—Is this the first dive you've filmed since ...?

Aston's answer seems rehearsed. He maintains the good-humored, slightly overexcited tone used by all of the show's presenters and crew.

—Since my girlfriend took some time off, you mean? Yup, the first time. Just for you, Roma.

The camera zooms in on Roma's flattered face and then suddenly pulls back to a medium shot and pans across the surroundings.

—I think we're lost.

A few seconds later, they've reached a guerrilla training area, a facility typically run by amateurs in the peripheries. It's in bad condition. The trainees have to climb a ladder up the diving tower. It looks rusty and it sways in the wind. There are no safety nets or other safety precautions like in the city academies. Aston's camera zooms in on a boy who has climbed halfway, but is now taking a break to catch his breath. A girl in an outdated flysuit™ is already standing on the platform; her suit is too big and doesn't conform to her body or sit tightly against her skin. She takes a step towards the edge of the platform, but doesn't dare to jump.

—You can do it, the boy calls out from the ladder.

No coaches or other adults are anywhere to be seen. From afar, you can make out a tall figure at the entrance of the building complex, probably a security officer from *Casting Queens*™. A group of about ten children has gathered at the bottom of the tower to watch and is now chanting: Jump, jump, jump ...

When Roma, Aston, and the crew approach the tower, the children start to cheer. They wave into the camera and try to go up to Roma, who is shielded by several security guards. Aston reminds the children that Roma is ill and shouldn't be touched.

The girl on the tower steps back, gets a running start, and then stops just before the jump. She begins to tremble and crouches down in the middle of the platform. When the boy makes it to the top, he encourages her. In Aston's close-up, you can see him stroking her back and pointing down towards the camera. He reaches out his hand to help her get up. She shakes her head.

The boy shrugs, checks the fabric on his outdated suit, does a few warm-up exercises. Then he takes a running jump and dives without hesitation. His first form is a challenging double somersault, his movements are fluid and precise. He fumbles a little when twisting left and loses his balance, but recovers. Everything goes so fast that my mind can barely follow. He's already approaching the fall spot™ when he starts on another form; he seems to have completely overestimated the distance. You only hear the bang seconds after he's already lying on the ground, his body twisted, his head bleeding. Aston holds the wide shot.

—Zoom! Zoom! a crew member shouts from the background.

Roma is screaming. Aston turns to her. She has her hands up in front of her face, but when she sees the camera she lowers them.

—What a tragedy, she says.

At that moment, you first hear the girl screaming from the platform. Aston's camera follows the noise and zooms in. The girl is leaning over the edge and flailing her arms wildly.

—Hey, you hear Aston calling, watch out, you're going to fall!

Although the girl probably can't hear him at all, I'm reassured by Aston's voice.

A crew member mumbles in the background, you can hear Roma agreeing. The camera pans back to her. She looks controlled and professional.

—What a tragedy, she says again. It's clear that we'll have to cancel the rest of *Discoveries* for today. Please send your condolences to his loved ones. We've set up a mourning forum on our website. I've already posted the first entry. The boy's name was Win, Win Miller.

At this point, the live feed cuts off. The forum on the *Casting Queens*™ website already has over three hundred thousand entries with condolences and inspirational pictures.

When Aston comes home, Zarnee intercepts him at the door, just as I'd requested. The shock of the accident offers an opportunity to deepen his relationship with Aston, to increase his influence. To encourage them to work together more closely.

—I saw the *Discoveries* segment, Zarnee says. Fuck. Are you okay?

—How could you voluntarily live there for so long? Aston replies.

Aston seems tired. His activity tracker is displaying a low heart rate.

After the filming cut off, I followed his GPS to several bars. Probably drinks with the crew. The bars were too crowded to get good visuals.

—Falls like that happen here, too, Zarnee says.

He follows Aston into his studio, I change the camera view. My eyes burn. It's 1:25 a.m.

—But not like that, Aston says. There were no safety precautions, nothing at all.

Aston's studio is messier than it was a few weeks ago. It's more like a living room than a photo studio. Takeout containers everywhere, half-empty bottles, clothes, discarded wrappers.

—I had a phase a few years ago, Zarnee says, when I walked through zone F every night.

Aston looks at Zarnee in amazement.

—What? Are you suicidal?

—Not at all. I've never felt more alive. The thought that a violent ex-criminal, still harboring the same instincts, could jump out of the shadows. A child molester, a murderer. I felt every individual atom in my body vibrating.

—Bullshit, Aston says.

He reaches for a plastic bag that's lying around and uses it to start collecting garbage from the floor. Zarnee pushes Aston's sleeping bag aside and sits down on the couch. He reaches for a photo portfolio that's resting on a side table and leafs through it.

—It was electrifying, he says. The risk. The possibility of a hand on my neck, a blade on my skin.

—How disappointing that no one ever really attacked you, Aston says sarcastically.

— How do you know that?

—Otherwise you wouldn't be here. Safe and sound.

Zarnee continues flipping through the photos without actually looking at them.

—Have you ever thought about not using filters on your photos? he asks. No post-processing? Just plain reality?

—If you're such a fan of plain reality, Aston says, why are you here now? Why not just stay in the peripheries? Take a walk through zone F?

Zarnee smiles and shrugs in a way that reminds me of Riva. Maybe it's the same for Aston, I can see the frustration on his face.

—I have to go to sleep now, Aston says. I have an early assignment.

Zarnee gets up and goes to the door.

—I envy you, Zarnee says, that you spent the whole day in the peripheries. I miss it. The heat, the noise.

—But you didn't have to relocate. And take a place away from someone who really wants it.

Zarnee nods and smiles at Aston before he leaves. In the doorway, he stops to wave.

I watch Zarnee walk over to the window wall in the living room. From a distance, you could mistake his silhouette for a woman's body. A person like a fish, adaptable, agile. His charisma is palpable, almost tangible. It reminds me of Andorra, her presence when she came into a room. How she made the people around her look indistinct, colorless, only half exposed. The way classmates gathered around her in a natural way. Maybe that's one reason why I still think about her, why I can't forget her after such a long time.

23

A loud noise in Riva's apartment. I run from the bathroom to the screen without washing my hands.

Riva is sitting on the sofa, Zarnee is next to her, knee to knee. She's holding the wooden thing that Zarnee brought with him when he moved in. She presses it with her thumb, it makes a loud crunching noise, I wince. The object in Riva's hand is now star-shaped. I wish she would get rid of it; the sound echoes inside my skull. She strokes the wooden surface with her index finger as if it were a living thing.

—I never met my biofather, Riva says, but I did meet my biomother. She lived with me for two years, I read that in my file. I don't remember her, but sometimes I feel like I might be able to if I try. That I just have to dig deep enough.

She tries to see Zarnee's face, but he's looking out the window.

—This morning I suddenly had a feeling like that, she says. I woke up and felt a hand on my cheek. I thought it might be you or Aston, but no one was there. I closed my eyes again and gave in to the feeling. A hand stroking my cheek. And then a feeling of warmth, as if a body had wrapped itself around me and kept me warm all around. Like you described in your blog. It could have been a memory of her like that. My biomother. Right?

Zarnee doesn't look at her. His gaze is fixed somewhere out the window, as if he were afraid to look her in the eye.

—Maybe, he says.

She touches his cheek with her right hand, as if to snap him out of a trance. He doesn't react, doesn't turn towards her.

—And what if a breeder gave birth to you? Would you also want to remember her then?

—A breeder didn't give birth to me, Zarnee. That would be in my file.

—Do you think it would make a difference?

—It probably would.

—Why?

—Because it would be a different relationship, wouldn't it? You know that best. You spent your whole life with your bioparents.

—So you think a breeder kid is already defective by the time it's born? Less human?

—I didn't say that. I just thought you might understand why I want to remember my biomother, who conceived me, carried me, and gave birth to me, and who was there with me for another two years.

—And I do. I'm sorry. I understand that.

—That was all.

—Okay.

—I'm sorry.

—You don't have to be sorry.

He puts his head against her neck and leans into her as if to test her resistance. It takes a moment for her muscles to soften and give in to the physical contact. I see them breathing with the same rhythm.

—I never used to think about the past, Riva says, only about the future and my competition goals. I never thought about death either. Not even if another diver had an accident. It seemed so abstract to me.

Zarnee sits up and looks at her.

—Now I feel like I'm trapped between my past and my future and they're closing in on me. Crushing me. Do you know what I mean?

—I think so.

She sinks back in his direction so slowly that the movement isn't visible in the gray evening light. Two images, one after the other without a transition. The first: two slender, upright figures. The second: a single figure. Impossible to distinguish where she ends and he begins.

Zarnee, I dictate a message, *take advantage of this closeness. Remind her of diving.*

Zarnee needs a moment to react to the vibration from his tablet.

—I'd love to see you dive again, he says, when he's back in position, leaning against her.

—Okay, Riva says. Maybe I'll dive for you sometime. I'll think about it.

I highlight the sentence yellow and send Masters a link to the video. *Karnovsky expresses motivation to resume training*, I write, *her willingness to communicate is greatly increased.*

Masters answers quickly: *Very good. Have the field agent set up an initial training appointment as soon as possible.*

24

The live feed isn't working. Transmission interference on the security cameras in Riva's apartment. The technician's analysis didn't uncover any software malfunctions. I had to tell Zarnee to check the hardware when Riva was in the shower. Apparently, he was able to fix the problem, but Masters ordered a security check before the cameras were unlocked again. He suspects Zarnee of sabotaging the cameras. When I checked the archive videos from the time before the outage, I couldn't identify any suspicious behavior.

I get up, walk through the room, stand by the window, observe the city at night. The lights in the apartment windows, the headlights moving in pairs along the street at the same speed. I have the urge to leave my apartment. Normally, I would hold back, stay on the ball, walk in place in front of the monitor to keep up with my minimum daily physical activity.

Instead, I put on my coat, take the elevator downstairs, and leave the building without knowing where I actually want to end up. I go in any direction my body takes me. I let my footsteps get faster and longer until I feel exuberant, almost cocky. I let the streets and houses blur in front of me, their rows of headlights and neon signs become glimmering flares in the night. I imagine Riva on the diving platform at the top of a skyscraper, jumping off, flying. Soaring up above the building and into the sky before diving back down again. A record-breaking attempt. I see the wide-eyed commentators, Dom Wu's tense face, and then Masters nodding happily in my direction.

I suddenly find myself standing in front of the same bar where I ended up a few weeks ago. This time I go in without hesitating.

It's more crowded than last time. Loud music, retro hits. I order a flydive™, correct myself immediately, and then order a vodka martini instead. The bartender seems to recognize me. He smiles at me.

—Why don't you just have a flydive™ if it's always the first thing you think of?

—You don't go with the first man you see. You go with the one you really like.

—But maybe the first man you saw is actually the one you always liked without realizing it.

—Vodka martini, please.

He starts mixing my drink and turns to another customer sitting at the other end of the bar.

I look around for the woman in the evening dress, wondering if I would even recognize her without it. I don't see anyone that reminds me of her. No one seems to be here alone; all of the guests are gathered in small groups, standing and sitting in different parts of the room, having conversations. The only person sitting alone is the man at the other end of the bar. When the bartender turns to bring me my drink, the man looks around the room. It's Royce Hung. He doesn't seem to recognize me. His eyes casually wander past me like any other customer here.

I finish my drink and order another martini.

The bartender looks at me approvingly and pours me

another. I pay, take my drink, and walk to the other end of the bar. I turn to Royce as if I had just noticed him from the corner of my eye.

—Royce Hung, I say. He looks at me, puzzled.

—Excuse me?

—Hitomi Yoshida.

I put my hand out to shake.

—We met through MattersOfLife™.

—You must have me mistaken for someone else, Royce says, turns away from me, and waves over the bartender.

—Royce Hung, I say, you are Royce Hung after all. Or at least you're registered under that pseudonym.

—You're mistaken, Royce says, sorry.

—We spent a whole evening together.

—Sorry.

The bartender puts a fresh beer in front of him on the counter.

—What are you doing, Royce? You could just tell me you didn't like the date. But ignoring my messages and pretending you don't recognize me is unprofessional.

—I don't know you, Royce says. Have a nice evening. His voice sounds deeper than I remember it.

He holds up his beer bottle to cheers, then he turns to his tablet on the bar and starts scrolling through content. I look at him. I'm absolutely sure it's Royce Hung. I remember his face clearly from when he bent down to kiss me.

—You too, I say, have a nice evening. Fuck you.

Before he can say anything back, I've already left the bar. I lean against the wall next to the entrance. The martini glass is still in my hand. My body is trembling violently. I'm shaking so intensely that the martini spills on my blouse. I drop the glass, it shatters on the asphalt, and then I start running. For a moment, I close my eyes and run into the darkness. Suddenly, I hear the sound of screeching brakes and honking horns, I open my eyes and realize that I ran onto the road. I jump back and make an apologetic gesture towards the drivers. They continue their journey. I hope that no one notifies security services. So many credits would be deducted for endangering street traffic that I'd risk relocation to the peripheries.

The peripheries. When we weren't taken directly to the casting halls, they would have us walk two by two through the surrounding residential area. Everywhere, swarms of children, like wasps. Dirty and wild, unlike me and the other kids from the institute. They scared me, I tried not to touch them, clinging to Andorra's hand.

Later, I saw them in the audience, screaming and clapping. Today casting audiences are all simulated; at that time, there were still live spectators, particularly children, a chaotic crowd. They seemed violent to me, I knew that I couldn't defend myself if they came up to me and threatened me. It sent a shiver down my spine to think of living among them, indistinguishable like them. What if my bioparents lost their jobs or if I failed my exams and had to give up my place at the institute? I imagined myself being driven to the peripheries. How they would push me out of the van, into the chaos.

We had to wait in front of the casting halls for the security check before they let us in. A child was playing near me. I couldn't help but stare at it. You couldn't tell if it was a girl or a boy. It was maybe three years old and stuffed in a sack-like outfit that was torn in some places. It looked as if the child were packed in a shopping bag. He or she picked at the holes in the fabric, you could see brown skin through them. Rolls of baby fat. At some point, it plopped down and lay back in the dirt. It stretched its arms and legs out to both sides, made flying movements, laughed. Its curly hair on the dirty, sandy ground.

I had to throw up. The children in my group backed away from me. A supervisor came over to clean and disinfect me before we entered the hall.

25

The normal split screen is back up on the monitor, but it looks almost as if the wrong apartment was activated. There are people everywhere. Electronic music is blasting from the sound system, which hasn't been used since the start of this job. Two young men are sitting cross-legged on the floor, Zarnee is deep in conversation with two women on the sofa. Riva and Aston are nowhere to be seen.

I click my way from camera to camera, but Riva isn't there. My right temple starts throbbing.

Where is Riva? I write Zarnee.

He glances at his tablet when my message appears and then puts it down on the sofa.

Zarnee? Where is she? I write.

Zarnee looks down at the device, smiles, and then turns in the direction where he suspects I might be watching from a camera. He puts his hand up and gives the peace sign.

One of the young women next to Zarnee is styled in the kiddie-look™. Her eyes are made up to look big, her skin is whitened with powder, her cheeks are covered with apple-sized red powder circles. Her mouth resembles a red painted fish mouth, small and round. She's wearing a blue and white dress with a sailor collar. Her white stockings are pulled up over her knees. She's leaning on Zarnee

like a child on her father. It's a strange image, considering how much Zarnee looks like a child himself. Then
again, amidst his entourage, he seems like a tribal leader
or cult guru. His thin arms draped around the shoulders
of his sheep.

They're all fixated on their tablets; from time to time
they react to the content with giggles or gasps. Zarnee
keeps looking up from his device and observing his
guests. Every now and then he brushes a strand of hair
from the forehead of one of the two girls and is rewarded
with a smile or a kiss on the cheek.

Zarnee, I write. *Answer my question.*

Zarnee looks down at his tablet again, reads, smiles.

Then he lowers the volume on the sound system.

—When you release sheep into the wild, he asks them,
do they need a shepherd to survive?

Everyone laughs. One of the boys raises his hand for a
high five.

—Cyeoym, says the girl in the kiddie-look™.

I find several entries for the word, including things
like the product code for a tablet cover and a username.
The most likely answer is that it's an acronym for *close
your eyes, open your mind.* My facial-recognition search
shows that the two women and one of the men live in the
peripheries and are only allowed in the city for work.
They must have crossed the border with a fake call sheet.
Masters won't like that.

I check the display every time I get a notification on my
tablet. Zarnee still hasn't responded. Instead, my tablet
continuously beeps with news alerts, advertising messages, and notifications from the PsySolutions server
about new evaluations in the tracking tool. My temple
throbs. Before I even finish logging it on the pain scale,
the pain increases so much that I have to adjust the entry.

I mute the notifications for a minute and concentrate on my breathing.

The pain spreads from my right temple to the entire back of my head. I take an ice pack out of the freezer and hold it against my temple. Then I take two pills and lie on the floor. First I lie on my back and, when that doesn't help, in child's pose. I kneel on the floor, my forehead pressed against the cool vinyl. For a moment, I manage to concentrate completely on my breath. The headache subsides a little. I stay like this for five minutes, then I slowly stand up.

Everything on the monitor is still the same as before. The girls next to Zarnee on the sofa, the boys sitting cross-legged across from them. Zarnee still hasn't answered my message.

Zarnee, I write. *We have a contract. I want to know where Riva is.*

This time he considers my message for a bit longer than before. Again, he turns in the direction where he suspects I'm watching and holds up his middle finger.

Wrong camera, I write. Zarnee laughs when he reads it.

—What's so funny, the girl on his left asks.

—Life.

She laughs and leans against him.

For a while they sit there like that. They're all absorbed in their gadgets except for Zarnee, who's looking out the window, preoccupied. He finally reaches for his tablet.

I get his message immediately: *She's out. That's all I know. She's a free person. Isn't that what you wanted? That she get out more?*

When I don't react, he adds: *Which is the "right" camera?*

I don't answer. Zarnee turns towards the main camera, smiles, and gives me the finger. Probably a coincidence.

—What are you doing? the girl next to him asks.

—I'm exercising my freedom of expression.

The girl turns in the same direction and copies his gesture. The others follow.

I hope Masters isn't logged in. It occurs to me that the notifications are still muted. Over three hundred have accumulated on my work monitor. Almost sixty new files in the data archive. Messages from my assistant, who was following up on information requests. Masters worked on ten of my documents and sent me three messages. The newest one is seventy-five seconds old.

It's nice to see you have your little actor so under control.

I don't know how to respond.

Have you noticed that three of the people present are on the watch list under suspicion of spreading propaganda? Masters writes. *Are you involved in subsidizing an underground organization, Ms. Yoshida?*

In my most recent performance reviews, Masters criticizes me because Zarnee often doesn't respond to my requests and has specifically ignored my request to persuade Riva to return to diving or at least regular fitness training. In the staff rankings, I'm back in the middle group after briefly skyrocketing to the top at the start of the intervention.

I will instruct the field agent not to allow such people into the apartment, I answer.

The kiddie-look™ girl has started to cry. Her makeup is running and the red droplets on her white bib-style collar make it look like she's bleeding. Zarnee strokes her hair.

—Roma's condition has gotten worse, the girl says in a raspy voice. They're only giving her a few more weeks. The girl on Zarnee's right leans over to look at the tablet. Then they hug each other.

They seem harmless to me, I write Masters. *You don't think so? Totally normal teenagers.*

—Let's be grateful for the time we have left with her, one of the boys says.

At that moment, Riva comes in through the apartment door. She seems transformed. There's a spring in her step and a cheerful expression on her face. This image matches the archive videos from the time before she resigned: multiple shopping bags on her left arm, a vitamin drink in her right hand. She greets everyone there and sits down next to the boys. Her behavior suggests that she already knows the visitors, which can't actually be the case.

My tablet vibrates with an urgent-message™. The technical service has finished assessing the camera malfunction in Riva's apartment. The hardware was not sabotaged; it was an internal problem with the data transfer between PsySolutions and the security company. The technician uploaded the video footage from the blackout. I quickly run through it.

At one point, I stop short. I see Riva dancing.

I skip back in the recording. Riva is alone in the living room, sitting on the floor, lost in thought. Suddenly, her upper body falls forward, she presses her right cheek to the ground, her arms next to her head, her fingers pressed firmly into the floor. Then she pushes off her hands and feet, lifts up, hits the ground again. She repels off the floor once more and then stops. She lifts her right leg into an arabesque, holds the pose for ten seconds, her muscles tightened, then she leaps across the room, turns, stops again. She starts again, jumps, makes a turn.

She smiles, her eyes are closed, her facial expression relaxed, almost blissful. Riva's body turns with full force, her leaps span almost the entire length of the room. She turns and jumps, repeating each movement several times, going through the positions she learned in Dom Wu's training program.

The sight is electrifying. Riva has resumed training. It's hard to believe.

I check the date and time of the recording. I almost want to ask the technician if he is sure that the material is not from the archive and was just tagged incorrectly. Riva's body dancing appears to me as an apparition, the resurrected spirit of a dead woman.

Riva's dance practice is interrupted when Zarnee comes in. He stands in the door for a moment without her noticing. When she eventually sees him from the corner of her eye, her body freezes, her face fills with shame.

—Don't stop, Zarnee says.

Riva laughs with embarrassment, shakes her head, and slides down onto the floor.

Zarnee sits next to her and looks at her from the side. Their hands touch.

—I can't imagine it, Zarnee says after a while, what it's like to dive. I never dared.

—It's hard to describe, Riva says. You're one hundred percent with yourself, the rest of the world fades away. At the same time, it's also a total out of body experience, that rush of adrenaline. It's the most beautiful feeling. You have it all and you can lose it all at any second. It's like being in love.

—Only more dangerous, Zarnee laughs.

—It's the only moment when I feel absolutely certain, says Riva, when I don't question anything. You follow your instinct, rely on your body. As if you've been playing a role for your whole life and then, at that moment, you transform back into yourself. It's how I imagine it feels to be a newborn baby again. Without any doubt.

—Then you should go back to it, Zarnee says. Riva nods.

—Maybe you're right, she responds.

My fingers are trembling as I send the link to Masters.

He writes back immediately. *Good work, Ms. Yoshida. In the weekly report, give a concrete prognosis for recovery that we can present to the investors. And get your field agent under control. We can't take any risks.*

I have to smile. My employee score will rise again today. The outlook is good. I want to enjoy the moment, but my headache is back. The tension in my neck has spread to my cheekbones. Maybe I've been clenching my jaw without realizing it, as I often do in my sleep. I get back on the floor and into child's pose.

I can hear the voices from Riva's apartment echoing through my apartment. Zarnee's guests are still there, talking and laughing. Riva's voice mingles with theirs as if she were always a part of the group.

With my eyes closed, it almost sounds like my apartment is full of people. I imagine that I'm surrounded by friends, sitting together, eating, talking, laughing. I concentrate on my breathing and do a visualization exercise. I'm in the institute lounge. A memory. Andorra is standing on the couch and playing the moderator of *Casting Queens*™.

—You're out, she says, you too, you too, you too. Hitomi, you won.

Everyone throws their arms around my neck. We dance around the couch. Andorra bows with the elegance of a ballerina.

—Thank you, thank you, my beloved fans. Thank you, thank you.

One of the boys plays a vj running after me on the street.

—What do you have to say about your victory, Hitomi? he shouts. How do you imagine life in the city? What district do you want to live in? How good do you think your chances are of making it? Where do you think you'll be in ten years?

Media Usage Log Archive No.: Bc17
Employee: @PsySolutions_ID5215d (Hitomi Yoshida)
Content: familymatters.org
Media Type: Blog
Safety Category: Questionable (watch list, propaganda)
Usage History Data: Frequency of use medium, average 4.5 times per day.

Recommendation from the Department of Media Security: Monitor use more closely, employee Hitomi Yoshida now blacklisted

Closed Caption Track: "Something Political Today.srt"
today its going to be political for once sorry people this is an exception for those of you who dont like politics just press stop um i always get so many questions from you that i still havent answered yet weather i think im a happier person because i grew up with my bioparents or weather i think im healthier because i was fed real mothers milk as a baby and so on um i never answered them before because its political and my blog actually isnt most of you read my blog because you want to switch off or you want to dive in to another world you dont know i under stand that too as a child i did nothing but watch glamour videos or blogs from VIPs or gossip sites because i wanted to imagine a life that i didnt have so i can under stand that well i also always felt like i couldnt really answer the questions because i have

nothing to compare my life with and im not an expert but now that the debate has just gone viral again i thought i had to say some thing surely youve all seen the post from future vision it actually says the usual stuff so most studies show that it makes no difference to your health if you grow up with your parents or within a facility and the naturals of course have said that the studies are all funded by companies that benefit from the results future vision responded by saying that if our way of caring for children is so harmful um then why arent most people criminally aggressive or at least somehow unbalanced the post said weve never had a more balanced harmonious and just society we all have the same goal and all the same opportunities we all grow up in the same facilities we all go to the same castings everyone who has achieved any thing has achieved it because of their personal performance and not because of special circumstances um i found it pretty convincing at first but maybe also because the naturals mostly get on my nerves with their negativity theyre always against every thing anyway or um well i dont want to say that theyre right with their neigh saying i mean youre all great people and youve all grown up in care facilities but on the other hand im just not sure if its all true with the same opportunities so dont get me wrong umm i really dont want to get political here its just so well how do you say im just in the unique situation with my family umm and i have a lot of friends who live in facilities and i already get the impression that there are differences and especially when i hear that there are facilities in the city that you can pay a certain amount umm and you get a special education and better chances of being accepted into the academies of course i dont know if thats true i can only say how i experience it and it doesnt seem fare to me um from my friends i know i am better off because i grew up with my biofamily and i mean theres a good reason why you check out my blog why its so popular how should i say it so i think there are certain differences and im also not one hundred percent sure if you can rely on these studies thats it from me i hope i answered all the questions the next time itll be happier again i promise ha ha until then ciao

26

Riva, Aston, and Zarnee are sitting around the coffee table as if they've been waiting for me.

All day, the apartment on the screen was empty. Aston was shooting in the peripheries, Zarnee and Riva were out in the shopping district. It didn't seem very productive for me to watch them shop, so I left my apartment for the first time in days to do an intense workout at a gym. I've gotten very out of shape. I saw a man raise his eyebrows when he saw my monitor readings. I was so ashamed that I spontaneously increased the minimum physical activity on my tracker by a fifth. I didn't stop training until Zarnee's GPS data on my tablet showed him approaching the apartment again.

It's an unfamiliar sight. Aston next to Riva on the couch, close to each other, Zarnee sitting across from them for a change. In their glasses, dark red liquid. In the background, easy listening at a soft volume. They're talking quietly.

At first I don't really listen at all. I let their quiet voices lull me in, blending with the music like white noise. I lean back and close my eyes for a moment. Riva's voice can be heard again and again. It's not just her physical condition that's being restored. Her general social demeanor has also been rapidly improving since Zarnee's arrival. Gestures and facial expressions have become much more reactive. Just a few weeks ago she wouldn't even touch her tablet. Now she consumes, comments on, and creates posts regularly again—at least with Zarnee and his friends. She still hasn't returned to filling her official apps and blogs with content. But, since the academy still has the rights to her media output, they're using the images and videos that Riva posts on Zarnee's friends' blogs as material for the apps. Since then, the number of users has risen sharply. The investors seem satisfied. Riva still hasn't resumed the official training program, but her motivation seems to be restored. I observed her doing dance routines in her apartment on two more occasions. Zarnee has agreed to persuade her to train at the academy by the end of the week.

Nevertheless, Masters continues to give my work mediocre scores in the tracking tool and his performance reports. The ratings sting, even if I know that they serve my motivation.

—So, you guys don't do it anymore? I suddenly hear Zarnee say loudly.

He bursts into laughter. Riva and Aston's eyes meet. Even though I missed the beginning of the conversation, it's clear they're talking about sex.

—No, Riva says.

—Why not? Zarnee asks.

—Yes, why not, Riva?

Aston looks at Riva, his expression is confrontational. Zarnee seems pleased with Aston's aggressiveness, claps his hands as if it were a successful performance.

Riva turns away and looks out the window, shrugs. Zarnee crawls around the living-room table on his knees, sits down at Riva's feet, caresses her right leg.

—Hey, he says, relax. Just kidding around.

She reacts to his touch immediately, her whole body

relaxes, sinks into his hand. It reminds me of the videos of the child whisperers at the breeding houses in the peripheries. Andorra and I liked watching them at the institute. Giving them a certain look or placing a hand on them would be enough to make the wild beasts tame again. Children that a normal person couldn't approach within fifty feet.

Aston gets up and walks towards the studio.

—Stay a little longer, Zarnee says. Now that the three of us are finally all sitting together.

—I'm tired, Aston says.

He looks genuinely tired. Rings under his eyes, his skin pale and grayish. His activity tracker indicates that he's slept an average of four hours a night in the last few days and has been on the move for at least eight hours a day. He must be busier with *Casting Queens*™ than expected.

—Come on, Aston, one more glass, Zarnee says.

—I have to get up early tomorrow.

Once Aston has disappeared into the studio, Zarnee sits in the empty seat next to Riva and she leans against him, puts her legs up. The image reminds me of a picture on Zarnee's blog. One of the many photos that show Zarnee as a little boy sitting next to his biomother. He's leaning against her, her arm wrapped around his body, she's looking down at him. The picture only has warm hues; the blue tones were most likely filtered out during post-processing. Zarnee and his mother both have the same earth-colored skin tone, which is linked in the spectrum of color associations with terms like cozy, warm-hearted, and peaceful.

—You're hard on him, Zarnee says quietly.

He pets Riva's head, which is now resting against the side of his chest.

—You think so?

—Yes.

She shrugs.

—Don't always just shrug like that. Riva looks at him, confused.

—Say what you really think.

Riva remains silent, but her concentrated facial expression suggests that she's thinking about what Zarnee said.

I consider sending Zarnee an assignment. Questions for Riva that are still outstanding. In the last few days he has only rarely responded to my messages.

Zarnee, I write, *give her a pinch in the side.*

The message makes him laugh. He winks in the direction of the camera closest to him. He seems to have located all the security cameras at this point. Then he pinches Riva in her side.

She screams and moves away from him.

—What the fuck?

—You have to get out of your head, Riva. You have to do something totally crazy again.

—For example?

—Let's go out. Let's go to the peripheries. I'll show you where I grew up.

I don't have a very good feeling about this. Masters won't like the trip, but I'll let Zarnee do it. Maybe the reality of the peripheries will remind Riva of everything she's built in the city.

When they leave the apartment, their presence lingers like a fingerprint. The glasses and half-empty wine bottle are still standing on the living-room table. There are still light depressions in the couch cushions from where they were sitting.

I'm tired and want to go to bed. I can easily imagine

the type of place that Zarnee will choose. One of the underground clubs that he regularly visits—he often posts early morning photos from his nights out on his blog. I track his GPS data, but I expect that he'll turn off his tablet like he always does when he leaves the city. Without GPS, it's hard to locate people in the peripheries because they're outside of Skycam range and there are very few security cameras.

Zarnee's GPS tracker shows them crossing the border. He left the device on. It's almost like a challenge.

I follow the two on their way through the unsecured terrain, where no live footage is available. They leave the car somewhere and seem to be roaming around aimlessly. The satellite pictures of the surroundings show undeveloped areas, densely overgrown, without paths. I wonder how they manage to progress so quickly there.

After forty-eight minutes, they move out of the thicket and towards the industrial area. I can barely keep my eyes open.

They're heading for a vacant building complex where, according to the data synchronization, several birth and death clinics had previously been located, but have since gone bankrupt or been relocated. The buildings are in good condition and most of the security cameras are still operational. It's possible that the complex is simply going to be renovated before new clinics are opened.

Some areas seem to have been converted into illegal living spaces by squatters. I can see signs of regular habitation. Mattresses and chairs, extension cords, portable hotplates. Certain walls have been spray-painted with Roman numerals and letters from an alphabet that the translation software doesn't recognize.

Zarnee's GPS dot moves inside the building. I click my way through the corresponding camera views and find them on the second floor in a former birthing room. All that remains of the previous furnishings is one hospital bed pushed against the wall. Zarnee is holding Riva's hand as she scans every corner of the room. Her movements seem hesitant.

A high-pitched cry comes from an adjacent room, Riva flinches, Zarnee continues unfazed. I find the camera in the next room at the exact moment that Zarnee enters. Riva stops in the doorframe. Unlike the rest of the building, this room is still in its original state. It's a nursery with about fifty tiny empty beds. When another cry comes from one of the beds near the front, I suddenly realize that three of them are actually occupied. The babies must be between one and two months old. As if the sound were contagious, the other two babies start crying. A figure emerges from a dark corner of the poorly lit room, a boy, about Zarnee's age. He bends over one of the beds and puts something in the baby's open mouth. Zarnee goes over to the next bed, bends down, and lifts a baby out. He holds it against his chest and rocks it back and forth. It immediately gets quiet again, you can only hear the babies breathing.

—Who are these children? Riva asks.

She hasn't moved from the doorframe.

—Breeder babies, the boy says. His facetag identifies him as Ace Schilling, nineteen years old, unemployed, poor performance values.

Zarnee gestures for Riva to come closer. Once she's standing next to him, he holds the baby out to her. Its eyes are closed, it looks like it's sleeping.

She doesn't take it.

—Don't be scared, Zarnee says, he doesn't bite.

—He can't, the boy laughs, his adaptation values are way too high, DNA guarantee.

When Riva doesn't react, Zarnee gently puts the infant back into his bed.

—Whose are they? asks Riva.

—Nobody's, Zarnee says.

—I mean, where do they come from?

The boy walks up to Riva and holds out his hand.

—Ace. Welcome, Riva.

Riva mechanically shakes the hand in front of her.

—Even these babies sometimes scream for no reason, says the boy.

—Let's hope, Zarnee says, that they're still screaming when they grow up.

I think about what Masters will say when he sees these recordings. Squatters with untagged babies that must have been stolen from a breeder facility. I would have to report them, initiate an investigation. Remove Zarnee from the intervention.

And destroy everything that we've accomplished.

Bring Riva back, I write to Zarnee.

I hear his tablet vibrate, but he doesn't react.

Zarnee, I write, *right now!*

Zarnee's tablet vibrates. He pulls it out of his pants pocket, skims the message, then opens the back of the device with a quick movement and takes the battery out. His GPS tag disappears from the map on my screen.

It's 3:30 a.m. Masters's last activity on the server is displayed at shortly after twelve. He still hasn't seen anything from the trip to the peripheries.

Without thinking, I log out of the security cameras and delete my access from the log.

Immediately afterwards, I realize what I've done. Removing work history data is not allowed. I've committed a criminal offense. My pulse shoots up. I feel like a casting candidate who has made a mistake on stage that can no longer be undone.

I remember the botched Call-a-Coach™ conversation. About how I deleted all the data without hesitation, without thinking.

I try to calm my breathing. No one ever noticed that the Call-a-Coach™ logs were deleted. Maybe nobody will notice anything this time either. The chances are good. They won't look for external recordings if I don't mention them in my daily report.

My pulse is slowly returning to normal. But there's still the inescapable feeling of intense disappointment. I'm disappointed in myself. How could I lose control like that?

I see myself as a young girl in the institute. I think of her achievement potential. Her hopes. Her dreams. Back when I was still able to do what was expected of me.

27

At night I dream about Masters. He's fused to my back like a tumor. His body compressed into a backpack-sized knot, his head in my neck, whispering criticism into my ear. I sit in front of my monitors and try to concentrate on the data analysis. Every time I click on a file, it multiplies. You halfwit, Masters whispers. She'll never dive again.

When I wake up, I'm sitting at my desk. I'm sure I fell asleep in bed.

On the work monitor, the securecloud™ folder with my performance reviews is open. It's empty. I restart the computer, log back in, open the cloud. The log indicates that the files were removed a few minutes ago by someone who entered my employee ID and password.

I don't remember deleting them. I try to recover the files, but they've also been removed from the backup. My fingers are shaking. Unauthorized removal of corporate documents, such as employee data, triggers a security alert by default. How am I supposed to explain this?

I remember Andorra and the strange sleep disorder she suddenly developed in her last year at the institute. How I woke up in the middle of the night because she was making a commotion in our room. She was digging through documents at her desk. There were sheets of paper and various objects lying all over the floor. I asked her what she was doing. She didn't answer. Even though her eyes were open, she didn't seem conscious. She let me lead her back to her bed and then went right back to sleeping normally. In the morning, I excitedly told her about her strange nighttime behavior. We laughed about it then, but when it happened again a few nights later it didn't feel right. I brought Andorra back to bed, waited for her to fall asleep, and didn't tell her the next morning. This nightly version of Andorra seemed like a clone to me, a strange being who had the same appearance and voice as Andorra, but only as a type of camouflage. As if someone had taken possession of her body and was controlling it for unknown purposes.

The notification sound from the internal messaging channel tears me out of my thoughts. It's an urgent-message™ from someone in our data security department.

According to the log, the following 67 sensitive internal files created by Hugo M. Masters were removed from the secure-cloud™ at 4:21 a.m. by your user profile without management approval. Please confirm that you are responsible for the deletion in order to rule out the possibility of hacking.

I suspect that I might have been sleepwalking, I write to the data officer.

You mean that you deleted the files in your sleep?

That seems to be the only explanation. I can't remember deleting them. But I woke up at my desk and the files were gone.

I'll run the security scanner on your server to rule out a hack.

Okay, thanks.

I reported the incident to management. They'll contact you.

Okay. Can you recover the deleted files?

Already done.

Thank you.

I write a note to Masters about the incident. He'll be less angry if I tell him myself than if he learns about it from the internal communications department. To my surprise, he answers immediately. It's 4:26 a.m.

Come for a medical examination first thing tomorrow morning.

This has really never happened to me before. I'm very sorry. It was not intentional.

All the more reason to have a medical exam.

I have a compulsory check-up at the end of the week anyway.

Come tomorrow morning.

Okay. I'm really sorry, Mr. Masters.

Go to sleep. Your sleep habits are far too irregular. And you didn't meet your exercise minimum again.

I'm sorry, Mr. Masters.

Go to sleep.

But I can't get back to sleep. I think about Andorra before she disappeared. How she was possessed by a foreign entity that stripped her of her passion for life. How it turned her into a sad figure, unpredictable and dangerous.

We sat on the bed and watched *Casting Queens*™. We laughed and commented on the performances and the jury's statements. Suddenly, Andorra jumped up like she was in pain.

I asked if something had bitten her. Even though the windows were covered with mosquito nets, they somehow always found a way in anyway. She shook her head and stared at me, not responding to my questions. At some point I just went back to watching the show. One of our favorites had made it to the second-to-last round. She wanted to be a judge. The tasks were specific to her chosen profession, revolved around legal texts, the main principles of the legal system, and the constitution. The candidate answered the questions so quickly that I could hardly follow and had to stop the stream from time to time and repeat parts. I was so absorbed in her performance that I forgot about Andorra.

All of a sudden she was standing right in front of me. She shook me as if I needed to be woken up. She pushed my tablet off the bed and yelled at me:

—You're an idiot, Hitomi, you're a dumb, stupid animal. You don't care about anything! You don't understand anything!

I was so blindsided that I couldn't say a word. I began to cry. Never before had Andorra spoken to me like that.

I looked at her, the girl I had been with my entire life, who had slept beside me every night for as long as I could remember.

There was a stranger in her place. Crying made my mucous membranes swell. The tears seemed to spur on Andorra's anger.

—Where do you think she'll end up if she doesn't make it to the next round? she snapped at me.

—Then she'll try again next time, I said.

—And if she doesn't make it then?

—Then she'll try again.

—You don't get it!

She spit the words from her lips like shards of glass. I had never seen her so upset.

—What don't I get, Andorra? What do you want from me?

—You pretend that there are rules that apply to everyone. But it's not a level playing field! When we go to the castings, we always cut straight to the final rounds. Haven't you ever noticed?

—Because we've been pre-qualified.

—But how did we get pre-qualified, Hitomi? What makes us so special?

—We got good results in our preliminary exams, we perform better than the others.

—Do you really believe that? Andorra asks.

—Why not?

She shook her head and left the room. That night she didn't sleep in her bed.

I didn't see her at breakfast the next morning either.

The first time I saw her again was in class, freshly showered and in her uniform like everyone else. When I hesitantly sat down, she smiled at me as if nothing had happened. She whispered in my ear that she hadn't done the math assignments. She would get points taken away and have to do additional make-up work. I was so grateful to have my friend back that I just erased what had happened between us. I never wanted to think about it again. I said I would help her with the additional assignments so that she could finish them faster. She smiled.

—You're the best, she said.

28

—You need to move more.

I can only see the outline of the doctor's face in front of the bright sun shining in through the window wall. A few spots around the eyes, everything else is covered in shadow.

—Ten thousand steps a day, he says. That's the contractual agreement. You never made it past four thousand last week.

—I can't always leave my work monitor. I'm doing a live analysis.

—Then exercise in the office. Your health should be close to your heart. The fitness requirements aren't in place to serve us, they're for your own good.

I nod and try to make him feel like I'm going to follow his instructions, that I'm going to do a better job in the future.

—Your sleep is very irregular.

—It's difficult at the moment, yes.

—A regular sleep rhythm is essential for physical and mental health.

—I know.

—I'll prescribe you a stronger sleeping pill. You should do relaxation exercises thirty minutes before falling asleep. We have several app suggestions on the server.

—Okay.

The doctor speaks into his tablet. His voice is deliberately quiet. I'm afraid it's a bad evaluation.

—Do you think that the lack of sleep is what caused my somnambulism? I ask as nonchalantly as possible once he's finished with his notes.

—It wasn't somnambulism, Ms. Yoshida.

—What do you mean by that?

—We analyzed the data from your activity tracker. It couldn't have been sleepwalking because you were awake when the company data was deleted.

—But I woke up in front of the monitor.

—Data doesn't lie, Ms. Yoshida. You know that just as well as I do.

—I assure you that I didn't intentionally delete the files.

—Ms. Yoshida, you're the expert: doesn't it make sense that an employee who repeatedly receives average to poor performance reviews would want to delete them in order to improve her performance fee?

The doctor smiles in a deescalating way, just as I learned to do in crisis training. I recognize the contrast between his natural-looking expression of empathy and his analytical gaze. He's trying to assess my reaction to the confrontation.

—I can only tell you what I remember, I say. And I didn't wake up until the data had already been erased.

—I believe you perceived it that way, Ms. Yoshida. Sometimes our brain blocks memories that we can't process. As I said, you're the expert.

What if I really was completely conscious when I deleted the data? If it was a sudden attack and now my mind is protecting me from the awareness that I would do such a thing? If my deleting the camera data from the birthing clinic and the Call-a-Coach™ conversation were signs of a destructive inner process? A kind of loss of control over my consciousness? Over my thoughts, my behavior? I suddenly feel like I'm falling, and have to support myself against the edge of the examination table next to me.

As a child, I trained myself to play through all possible outcomes before reacting to anything. Before each word, I considered its potential effect on the other person.

—Ms. Yoshida, the doctor says. We would like to give you another chance.

It perfectly fits the tone that's recommended for un-cooperative clients. Caring, but firm.

—Mr. Masters has decided not to press charges against you.

—Thank you. Thank you very much.

The relief can be heard in my voice. I'm starting to feel woozy.

—Take it as a warning. We reserve the right to take legal action if you don't comply with your contractual obligations in the future.

—Of course, I say. That's not going to happen.

—That includes your health requirements. You need to make sure you get enough exercise. Sufficient sleep.

—Yes, I say.

—We only want the best for our employees.

—Yes, I say. Thank Mr. Masters very much. Please tell him I'm sorry.

When I go to leave, the doctor gives me a friendly smile, shakes my hand, and then immediately disinfects his own hand afterwards. In the hall outside his office, I'm overcome by the sensation of falling again. My vision is so blurry that I have to lean against the wall.

29

—I have to tell you something.

Zarnee seems nervous. Fidgeting in place, constantly touching his right ear.

—Did something happen? Riva asks.

—Sit down.

Zarnee takes Riva's hand and leads her to the sofa, pushes her onto the cushion, sits down next to her.

—Zarnee, you're scaring me.

—There's nothing to be scared of.

I immediately get a bad feeling.

Zarnee, I write him via our communication channel, *what are you doing?*

The notification sound makes Zarnee look over at his tablet on the living-room table. He reaches for it, glances at the screen, and then switches the device to silent. His facial expression doesn't indicate whether he has read my message.

—Riva, Zarnee says.

He clasps her hands. In the full shot, they almost look like a couple, their eyes focused directly on each other.

—I'm leaving, Zarnee says.

—Where? Now?

—I've already packed my things.

—What do you mean?

—I'm not coming back.

Zarnee? What are you doing?

His tablet vibrates, but he doesn't even look.

—What do you mean? Riva asks again. Her voice is breathy and quiet.

—I'm moving out.

Zarnee, I write, *end the conversation immediately and call me.*

Zarnee holds Riva's hands in front of his face as if he wants to make sure that they're real.

—I'm sorry, Riva.

—What happened? You don't have enough credits? Are you being expelled?

—Something like that.

Zarnee! End the conversation!

—It's just …

His voice breaks off.

—I'm ashamed to tell you, you understand, he says.

—You can tell me anything.

—I'm not who you think I am, Zarnee says, or at least not exactly. I didn't just move in here. It was an assignment.

My activity tracker starts beeping. A heart-rate warning. My pulse is racing. I take slow, deep breaths to try to calm down, while simultaneously sending Zarnee an onslaught of instructions that he ignores. My tracker doesn't stop beeping. I rip it from my arm and throw it across the room.

—What do you mean by assignment? Riva asks.

Zarnee doesn't answer, he takes the tablet and seems to be skimming through my messages. I type as fast as I can, so that Zarnee reads what I write before he puts the tablet down again.

You signed a non-disclosure agreement! You'll be expelled for breach of contract.

I see Zarnee laugh.

—Talk to me, Riva cries. What's going on? He takes her hands and kisses them.

—Listen, he says, give me a second. I just need a minute to get rid of a mosquito that's buzzing around my nose.

He starts typing.

I don't have a contract. Masters fired me.

My activity tracker beeps again. A warning that I've left it off for too long.

That can't be, I write.

Check your facts, mosquito.

I check the server, Masters is offline. I dial his number and get an out-of-office message.

Even if it's true, I write, *the confidentiality agreement still stands. You can't tell her, you'll ruin everything. You'll ruin Riva's chances at getting better.*

—Zarnee, Riva says, tell me what's going on!

Riva was never sick, Zarnee writes.

The warning sound from my tracker just won't stop. I pick it up and put it on again. My heart rate is still too high. I want to mute the tracker, but I'm so panicked that I can't find the settings.

Masters isn't responding to my urgent-messages™.

—I was hired by a company, Zarnee says.

—Why? Who?

Please Zarnee. Don't ruin my project.

Zarnee skims my message from the corner of his eye.

He laughs and shakes his head.

—A company that Dom hired. Your sponsors are paying for the intervention. I'm supposed to make you productive again.

I'm overwhelmed by a feeling of powerlessness. I have the urge to turn the monitor off and on again, to restart the cameras. To start over.

How cold my apartment is. I have goose bumps all over my body. The tracker is beeping incessantly. My heart rate has risen to one hundred and sixty. I cling to the table to maintain consciousness. I have to breathe calmly. Think calmly.

—I don't understand at all, Riva says. What are you supposed to do? Dom hired you?

She lets go of Zarnee's hand and crosses her arms in front of her chest.

—I wasn't supposed to do anything in particular, Zarnee says. The psychologist had this theory that my influence, my presence could have a positive effect on you.

—Why?

—Because you wrote about the peripheries in your diary app. They probably thought we would get along because of my blog. They weren't wrong.

—Dom read my diary app? Riva moves away from Zarnee on the couch.

I keep dialing Masters's number. My heart threatens to explode. Just a panic attack, I tell myself. It's all in your head.

As I'm writing him another message, I get a notification that Zarnee has blocked me.

—The company that Dom hired decrypted it, he says.

—They can't do that.

—You gave up any right to privacy when you signed your contract with the academy, Riva. Everything you write during your employment period belongs to them.

—What else? asks Riva angrily.

—I'm not sure. But they're watching you. On the security cameras. They're watching us. Right now at this moment. A psychologist has been writing me messages.

He holds out his tablet to show her. She shakes her head.

An alert sounds on my tablet. Someone is at reception in my apartment building. Masters appears on the security monitor. I buzz him in.

Riva is crying. The white surface of the sofa is like a chasm between them. He seems unsure about whether he can approach her, touch her.

Pounding on my front door.

When I open it, Masters storms in. He is beside himself, his face is red and blotchy. Sweat is running down his cheeks from both temples.

He stares at me for a moment, as if he has to reactivate his ability to speak. I try to see what's happening on the monitor from the corner of my eye. I hear Riva crying.

—How could this happen?

Masters's whole body is tense, fingers clenched, shoulders hard and square. His posture is so aggressive that I instinctively take a step backwards and hold my arms in front of my body.

—Mr. Masters, I say, I tried to stop him. There was nothing I could do.

—I've been telling you from the very start that this man is a ticking time bomb! You ruined the project. The investors will jump ship.

—He said you fired him today.

—I tried to get rid of him before it was too late. Apparently it was already too late.

—But his behavior is a direct reaction to the termination. Why didn't you inform me?

—I had doubts from the beginning about whether he was the right person for the job.

—It did work after all. She was rehabilitated within a very short time.

—She is not one step closer. She's not diving. All she does is waste time with shady characters in shady establishments. The relationship with your field agent has drawn her further away from us than ever before.

On the screen, the full shot shows Riva on the couch. She's sitting upright and still, as if posing for a photo. Zarnee is nowhere to be found.

—Mr. Masters, I say, let me try to salvage the situation. Let me get in direct contact with Riva.

—You won't do anything, Ms. Yoshida. You're suspended until further notice.

—Mr. Masters. I promise you that I'll do everything in my power to get the situation under control. At least let me try.

—You're suspended from this moment onward. Failure to observe the rules will be punished with fines or punitive measures. Come to my office tomorrow morning. My assistant will send you the appointment. And mute your damn tracker. Your heart rate is way too high. Stick to your training plan and do your mindfulness exercises for once.

As I watch Masters step into the elevator on the security monitor, the strength leaves my body. I let myself slide down onto the floor. I try to focus my eyes on a specific point on the ceiling in an effort to avoid losing consciousness. The tracker finally stops beeping. My heart rate has dropped.

In the abrupt silence, I hear Riva crying. The monitor shows her in the same place on the sofa, but hunched over, collapsed. Her body shakes to the rhythm of her sobs. She seems smaller than before. The sight of her triggers a physical reaction in me, my heart rate starts to rise again, my stomach contracts and feels empty.

I click my way through all the cameras, but Zarnee has left the apartment. His tablet and his suitcase have disappeared. My facetag search for him delivers no results.

He'll be on his way to the peripheries, off the grid.

It's not worth looking for him. No punishment can harm him if he's already decided against the city.

But for Riva it's not too late. Riva is still there, in her apartment, on the sofa.

I think about going to her. To explain the situation. To persuade her to cooperate.

But I can't defy the suspension if I don't want to end up in the peripheries myself. I can only hope that Masters will give me another chance. I activate the training mode on my activity tracker and start my mindfulness exercises. I'll do the double session to prove to Masters that I'm serious.

30

Masters's office has changed once more. The Buddha statue is gone and he has furniture again. But the new office furniture is made of Plexiglas, so that you can see straight through it with just a little distortion. Masters is standing behind his desk, which makes parts of his stomach appear slightly wider than the rest of his body.

—Clearheadfurniture™, he says when he notices me staring. The CEO complained that you can't sit properly in my office. He's been having back problems lately. I chose acrylic because it has the same basic effect, don't you think? You can still feel the expansiveness of the space, both internally and externally. The absence of disruptive objects.

I nod as if I agree with him.

—Ms. Yoshida, Masters says, coming out from behind his desk. I spoke to your doctor this morning. Your fitness values and the results of your latest compulsory exams are worrying.

For a moment I'm confused because Masters didn't immediately start talking about the disaster from the previous day. I assume he's following an outlined progression in which he gradually approaches the topic in steps of increasing urgency.

—I'm in the process of adjusting my sleep rhythm, I say. I've set myself the goal of doubling my physical activity quota and mindfulness exercises.

—You have a number of psychosomatic symptoms, Ms. Yoshida.

—What do you mean?

—In your pain log, you've cited different types of headaches. Migraines, shooting pain, visual disturbances. Also cramps in the stomach and lower abdomen. It sounds like a person who's unfit for work.

—It's not that bad. I have it under control. It usually passes quickly with medication. I only logged it for the sake of being thorough. I don't want to cover anything up.

—I've spoken extensively with the specialist, Masters says, and, in view of your psychosomatic symptoms, we're both of the opinion that you're not in acceptable condition for employment at this time.

I can feel my heart racing. Heat floods my upper body.

—We have to release you from your contract for your own safety, Masters says. In this state, you aren't fit to work as a psychologist.

—Mr. Masters, I say. I try to keep my vocal inflection as neutral as possible, while also talking over the roaring in my ears. I'm very sorry about what happened with Zarnee Kröger. I should've prevented it. But I knew nothing about his dismissal from the project.

—We're grateful to you for the work you've done so far.

—At least let me try to make up for it. There's been so much progress recently. Riva Karnovsky's condition has improved. She wants to dive again. The prognosis is very good, an appointment has already been arranged for training at the academy. Give me a week. A few days at least.

—We've assigned a colleague to oversee the project from here on.

—Mr. Masters, please. Give me another chance.

Masters smiles.

—We've prepared a generous severance package for you. We recommend that you seek treatment for your symptoms. I've enclosed a list of the best outpatient and inpatient institutions in the area. Get help, Ms. Yoshida. We're happy to contribute to the costs of your rehabilitation.

I feel sick. I try to fix my eyes on a specific point in the room. The beam of sunlight hitting the corner of the Plexiglas desk in front of the window. Refracted and split in two.

I take a deep breath and then exhale again. I look back at Masters.

—Mr. Masters, I say with a firm voice, I'm fine. I'm doing a good job.

—Your health is close to our hearts, Ms. Yoshida. It should be close to yours, too.

—Mr. Masters, I'm not ill. I made a mistake. But Zarnee Kröger's influence on Karnovsky was positive. The investors must also see that.

The corners of Masters's mouth are slowly shifting. His facade of well-meaning professionalism is starting to crumble. He glances over at a glass clock on the wall to his right.

—Our assignment is to enable Riva Karnovsky to compete again, he says, and we have not made it a single step closer to that goal. The investors understand your medical situation. They wish you all the best for the future.

—Give me at least one week, please!

—Ms. Yoshida, the personnel change has already been initiated.

Masters's eyes move away from me and through the

room. I feel my heart pounding against my chest. My fitness tracker is about to sound the alert.

—I want a second medical opinion, I say. I deserve that.

Masters's expression is ice cold.

—I have to warn you, Ms. Yoshida, he says. We can initiate proceedings against you at any time. You deleted sensitive company data, withheld information about illegal activities, and removed data from an external security camera from your history. Did you think we wouldn't notice? As a gesture of goodwill, we've decided against pressing charges. If you would rather lose your license than just this single contract, that's your choice. The data shows that your finances are not exactly stable. You live in a building category that you can't afford with your income. If you lose your license, you'll be on your way to the peripheries within a few days. Do you want that?

While Masters is speaking, I'm suffering from a sort of out-of-body experience. With every word, my consciousness moves a bit further away until I see myself from across the room, standing in the middle of Masters's office. From a distance, I watch him stand in front of me, smile at me, and hold out his hand. I hear him say something, but I can't tell what. The blood rushes into my ears like white water crashing down a mountain. And then I come crashing down. My legs give way, but I can still see both of us standing in space, as if only a part of my body is fainting, as if I exist in two states: unconscious and completely lucid. I observe myself slowly sinking to the ground in front of Masters. I see him bending down to feel my pulse. Watch him pulling my legs up at a right angle, as if he were performing a gymnastics exercise on me. He has evaluated and understood the situation.

He is acting with complete composure. A model student, implementing every action point from his manager training—trainings that I conducted myself for a while —a combination of affirmations and maneuvers that were repeated until the measures could be carried out intuitively.

I watch myself being brought back to consciousness, Masters methodically shaking my body. The space gains contour. The darkness, like a filter over my irises, starts to fade. An asymmetrical Plexiglas shelf slowly appears in front of me.

Masters is still holding my legs up at right angles. They feel dull, dead. I feel tiny stitches in my fingers.

Then Masters lets my legs slide slowly to the ground and places them at an angle. As if I were a doll, deposited like a toy in his office.

I feel feverish. I sit up. Unsteady, I slowly take off my jacket and then let my upper body drop again. Even though my heart is racing, I'm consumed by extreme exhaustion.

—I'll get you a glass of water, Masters says matter-of-factly.

A sentence from a crisis training that I could have conducted.

He comes back with a glass of water, which he holds up to my mouth with one hand while lifting my head with the other.

—Don't touch me.

My voice sounds weak and brittle. I straighten up. Masters leaves the glass to me. He seems relieved to be able to give up the responsibility.

—Are you feeling better?

—No. I don't feel better. You just sacked me.

My voice sounds like someone else's. The tasteless

choice of words and the angry tone make me uncomfortable, as if they hadn't come out of my own mouth.

—Strictly speaking, it's not a termination. It is an exemption from your contract on medical advice.

I push myself up from the floor and stand.

—One day, you'll see what I'm capable of, I say, following an impulse that I don't understand.

—Is that a threat? Masters says with a smile I can't classify. Please sign here.

He holds out a tablet with the lengthy legal release, non-disclosure agreement, and official termination of access to all company property. I press my fingers one by one into the designated fields.

Without looking him in the face again, I leave his office. I feel sick.

I hurry to the next bathroom and throw up into the sink. I'm ashamed of my weakness. I'm sure that Masters is watching me.

Standing in the bathroom, seeing my pale face in the mirror, I think of how often I've observed Riva in her bathroom. An unexpected wave of compassion comes over me. I see Riva sitting on her sofa and crying. The walls of the staff restrooms are all covered with tiles. I never wondered where the cameras might be hidden.

The thought of going home is nauseating to me. I feel hot. Instead of heading to the parking deck, I walk down to the lobby and out through the main entrance. The cold hits me as I step out of the revolving door; it's like walking into an invisible wall. An unannounced cold spell. It occurs to me that I left my coat hanging on the Plexiglas coat stand in Masters's office. My jacket is probably still on the floor, reminding him of my presence like a bloodstain. All I have on is a white blouse and a heathered gray skirt with pantyhose underneath. The shock of cold does me good, I suddenly feel very awake. I am glad to have the heat of the past few weeks behind me.

Then I start to freeze.

At the building entrance terminal, it hits me that my tablet and my key fobs for the office, my apartment, and my car are in my jacket. Without the key fob to the office, I have to buzz back in. The woman at the door doesn't understand what I'm trying to tell her.

—You work for PsySolutions?

—Yes.

—And you lost your key fob?

—It's in my boss's office. Hugo M. Masters.

—Mr. Masters left the building a minute and a half ago. He has out-of-office appointments and won't be back until tomorrow.

—Did he leave my jacket behind for me, maybe?

—Your jacket?

—My keys are in it. I left the jacket in his office with the key fob in the pocket.

The cold is settling into my limbs. I start walking in place to warm up.

—What's your name?

—Hitomi Yoshida. Maybe you can let me in while we figure this out? It's very cold out here and I don't have my jacket.

—Employee number?

I try reciting the number from memory. I don't succeed. My teeth are now chattering, so I can hardly speak clearly.

—Can't you identify me using facial recognition?

I give my date of birth, my address, and where I did my training for data synchronization.

—I found you, the woman says. It says you've been terminated. I can't let you in.

—I just want my jacket so I can go home. My car is still parked in the employee garage. I promise to leave the building as soon as I have the keys.

—I have to check with your supervisor first.

—Can you let me in while I wait?

The cold is making my fingers and toes numb. The woman stops responding. I start jumping up and down and rubbing my arms. A group of employees from another department approaches the entrance. I get in line.

—Excuse me, one of the men in front of me says, do you work here?

—Yes.

—Where's your key fob?

—I left it inside.

—We can't let you in. You know the safety regulations.

—I just want to get into the lobby. It's cold and I forgot my jacket.

The man blocks me until the rest of the group has disappeared through the revolving door. Then he shrugs and goes inside.

I try to see into the lobby through the glass door. A woman is standing right behind the entrance, looking in my direction. I wave, rub my arms, point to my blouse and then the door opener. The woman turns away and quickly disappears into the building.

The wave of anger comes over me as unexpectedly as the fainting spell in Masters's office. I kick the locked door. Drum against it with my fists. Again, I feel split in two: the figure at the door, pounding against the glass in a rage like a psychiatric patient, and a second person, calm but powerless, watching from a distance.

Banging on the glass makes less noise than expected.

A stabbing pain in my hands finally draws me back

into my body. I'm seized with fear. I turn around to see if security has already been called.

The plaza in front of the building is empty. As far as I can tell from behind the glass, the lobby is, too.

I turn around and start running. There's no one on the sidewalk but me, the rows of cars keep moving along the road next to me. It's midday traffic, so it's mainly delivery vehicles from the popular take-out places.

I run. My fear drives me. I imagine the security guards waiting for me in front of my apartment. I pass a skytrain station and step inside to warm up. The feeling very slowly returns to my hands and feet.

The station is full of people. It looks choreographed, how they move so quickly without getting in each other's way, only slowing down slightly to hold their tablets up to the access control sensors.

My tablet is in my jacket on the floor of Masters's office. I see myself standing in the station hall, an obstruction dropped amid the crowd. A foreign body. I can't stand here for long without attracting attention.

One of the sensor gates doesn't close properly. It must be defective. I walk towards it and push myself through the narrow opening without looking around. My heart is pounding, but no one seems to have noticed.

I try to keep pace with the commuters, but the platform I'm heading towards only has trains going in the opposite direction of my residential district. When I turn around, I collide with a woman in a courier uniform and then with a middle-aged man, his briefcase falls on the floor. I try to weave around the bodies, arms press against mine, fabric to fabric. I'm hot, I squeeze through to the wall without breathing.

When I finally get on the right train and sit down, my blouse is half hanging out of my skirt and beads of sweat have formed on my forehead. I try to straighten my hair.

When we reach my district, it suddenly occurs to me that I can't get into my apartment without my key fob. I get out and walk around aimlessly.

Again, I find myself standing in front of the bar, not realizing where I was going until I got there. I go in. There are only a few guests. No manager would hold a lunch meeting here. I look around and see people like me, people who've been made redundant, relegated, underperformers. Two men are seated close together in a corner, engrossed in conversation. Another is sitting hunched over at the bar. As I walk up to the bar, a woman comes out of the bathroom and sits down with the men in the corner. They don't seem to notice her.

The bartender recognizes me.

—Flydive™, no, martini, he says with a smile and starts making a martini.

—No, I say, today I'll have the flydive™. He shakes his head.

—Do you get the impression that I'm not working hard enough?

His tone is much too familiar, but I'm still grateful for it. At least someone who thinks well of me.

—I don't want to have anything to do with getting people to work anymore, I say, trying to imitate his friendly tone.

Although our closeness isn't real, I immediately feel better. Studies prove again and again how much influence mental exercises can have on real emotions. Visualizations, role playing, affirmations.

—Bad day? he asks.

He obviously wants to talk. He's probably been working since early morning and hasn't spoken to a reasonably healthy person since. Not that I'm healthy. According to Masters.

—You could say that, I say.

He puts my drink down in front of me, picks up his own, and then clinks glasses with me. I take a big sip of the flydive™ and then make a face almost immediately.

—Hey, the bartender says with feigned indignation.

—Sorry, I say, that was an emotional reaction. It's the association, not the drink. The drink is good.

Laughter comes from the sitting area. One of the two men has turned away from the other and is giggling with his hand in front of his eyes. The other is laughing loudly and patting him on the shoulder. The woman across from them is chuckling as if she had made the joke.

—Do you want to tell me what ruined your day? the bartender asks.

—Plexiglas furniture, I say.

—You're going to have to explain.

I gulp down the rest of my drink. The bartender gives me a knowing smile and starts making me a martini. He suddenly seems strangely familiar to me. The way his slender hands move back and forth between the shot glass and the ice cooler, the way he brushes away a curl from in front of his eyes.

—My boss filled his entire office with Plexiglas furniture. It's because his boss has back problems and wants somewhere comfortable to sit. It makes it look as if something is wrong with your vision. Everything is somehow distorted, widened, pulled upwards.

—And?

—Then I got sacked.

The strange word suddenly feels right.

The bartender slams the martini glass on the counter in front of me, so that the clear liquid splashes over the rim.

—This one's on the house.

I feel a sharp pang when I suddenly remember that I can't pay without a tablet.

—Fuck fuck fuck fuck.

—I wouldn't expect such a dirty mouth at first glance.

—I can't pay for my drink. I left my tablet in my boss's office.

—Oops.

—I just stormed out like that. I wasn't thinking.

—I'll cover you.

—My keys too. I can't get into my car or my apartment anymore.

—If you can wait until the end of my shift, you can come with me to my place.

The bartender winks at me. His offer takes me by surprise. The lack of ambiguity in the invitation makes me reluctant. I don't want to have spontaneous sex with a stranger. Even my one-night stands are always planned through the partnering agency and then I know the person's profile, their sexual preferences. But what are my alternatives?

The same exhaustion that came over me in Masters's office is coming back now. If not with the man behind the bar, where else could I go? I can't contact anyone.

There's also no one for me to contact.

—That's nice of you, I say in a polite tone that suggests distance.

—I'm a nice person.

—Okay, I say. I'll go to your place.

When the bartender walks me to his car at the end of his shift, the alcohol has taken hold of me. I'm in a good mood. When I look over at him from the passenger seat, I just have to smile. He grins back. He suddenly seems much younger to me. I also feel very young again, like when Andorra and I met men in bars a few times when we were fourteen. The youthful exuberance I felt then. Andorra's contagious laughter and the way her body moved when she was dancing with someone. I thought of what a privilege it was to be her friend. How sincere and pure my affection was for her. It wasn't until the morning that my guilty conscience caught up with me, the fear of getting caught. Of punishments, of bad references, of a lost future. I told Andorra that I wouldn't go with her again—until the next time she woke me up, giggling and pulling my hand through the silent institute and out into the night.

The city lights rush past me. The sudden thought that Masters isn't breathing down my neck anymore. No performance reviews. No fear of the color red in the tracking tool.

I lean back and stretch my arms over my head, move my body as if I were dancing. The bartender laughs. Andorra, the way she danced. Eyes closed, arms stretched out over her head. Small beads of sweat on her upper lip, in the groove between her curved nose and her slightly open mouth.

I lean over to the bartender and kiss him. He playfully pushes me away because he can't see the onboard monitor.

The ride takes a while and the warmth of the car lulls me to sleep. When I wake up, the vehicle is in park mode. The bartender touches my face.

When he gets out and opens the door for me, I'm hit with a wave of bitter cold air and a stench that makes me wince. It smells like rotten food, animal carcasses, dirt. I remember the smell.

—Where are we, I ask the bartender, who is holding out his arm to help me out of the car. Do you live in the peripheries?

—My credit score still isn't high enough for a relocation permit. But I'm close. It won't be much longer. I have two other low-pay-grade jobs in the city. Once I have a city address, I can apply for a higher pay grade.

I start choking, feel the stomach acid rising into my throat.

—Too many martinis?

He holds my hair back, but I don't want to throw up. I envision the child with its plastic dress full of holes and the splatters of vomit being cleaned from my clothes. I swallow the acid back down.

The bartender's apartment is in a crudely built housing settlement. The indistinguishable rectangular concrete buildings seem to multiply into infinity and the dull orange street lamps only light certain parts of the street.

He has his arm around my hip to support me. I don't feel good anymore. I have a headache. The nausea is rumbling around in my stomach.

Once we're inside his tiny apartment, he gives me a cheap beer.

—Are you sterilized? he asks.

I nod and start to undress. Sex seems inevitable. I've lost the sense of pleasure I felt in the car, but now I'm here, I've made the unspoken agreement.

—Could you act like you aren't? he asks.

I've read the literature about paraphilias like this, the men who intentionally sleep with non-sterilized women because the risk arouses them. They don't get themselves sterilized, either. Every time they have sexual intercourse, they risk losing their status, their credit score. They risk being expelled to the peripheries or losing any chance of ever leaving them.

—How do you imagine me doing that? I ask.

—Just say things like: I'm ovulating right now. Don't come inside me. Please don't. Stop it.

In my dating profile, I listed sexual fetishes of any kind as a deal breaker. I've always found fetishism creepy because it's just so hard to explain psychologically. Even if the fantasies can be traced back to decisive trigger experiences in every client story. Why the same experience would lead to fetishistic behavior in one person and not in another is impossible to determine with any certainty.

31

The bartender wakes me up at 6:12 a.m. He's wearing a uniform from a downtown courier company.

In the car, my body starts to tremble. My legs feel tired, my head cloudy. My vagina hurts. When he smiles at me, all I can think about is how he asked me to scream: Stop it, stop it, I'm not sterilized!

I ask him to drop me off at PsySolutions.

—If you don't get your things back, come by the bar, he says. My shift starts at two

I nod and try to smile. He kisses me for a long time before he lets me go.

—Don't forget to kick him in the balls, he says as I get out.

—What?

—Your boss.

I shake my head and walk towards the building entrance. From the corner of my eye, I see the bartender making a vulgar gesture, probably intended for Masters. Then he drives away.

The thought of standing in front of Masters in my condition makes me break out in a cold sweat. He will smell the alcohol and feel even more justified in his decision. Hitomi Yoshida, psychosomatic symptoms, faints in crisis situations, tendency towards alcohol addiction.

When I press the intercom, I hear the same voice as the day before.

—Ms. Yoshida? I've located your jacket. Mr. Masters handed it in and authorized you to pick it up. I'm letting you in now.

When the door release buzzes, I hesitate for a minute before entering the building.

The lobby is empty.

The doorperson is a middle-aged woman. The tiny wrinkles around her eyes can't be treated anymore at this stage. No one else is around. No Masters. No security guards.

She's the oldest employee I've ever seen in a company. For a second, I forget why I'm talking to her and just stare.

—I need your fingerprint for the log, the woman says, holding up a tablet.

I put my fingerprint in the designated field and take the jacket, my key fobs, and my tablet, all individually vacuum-packed in numbered plastic bags.

—Was there a coat, too? I ask.

—You didn't say anything about a coat.

The woman enters something into her computer.

—Brand and size?

I can't think of either.

—Just leave it, I say. Keep the coat. Maybe Mr. Masters can give it to his interior designer.

—Lost items are either given to charitable institutions or destroyed after the end of the collection period, the woman says.

In my car, I rest my head on the steering wheel and close my eyes. Warm air blows into my face from the vents. The tiredness sets in, takes hold of my body. I'm afraid of losing consciousness again, but I eventually surrender to the feeling and let myself fall.

I'm still in my parking spot at PsySolutions when I come to. I drive home. Everything in my apartment is the same as I left it the morning before. The untouched quality calms me. For some reason I expected a battlefield, cables torn out, missing computers and screens. Instead, no indication of my new status: UE, unemployed. Even my credit score is still the same. I suppose Masters hasn't reported my termination to the credit institutions yet.

My work screen is on standby. The first touch opens the usual windows. Then, a pang in the pit of the stomach. The live monitor's split screen is just empty black fields. There are error messages flashing on the work monitor: *There is no account associated with this user name. Connection to server terminated. The link "Karnovsky_Log_B75k.link" can't be opened because the original was not found.*

All files are blocked: the logs, the secondary data, the video archive of the live analysis. Along with my employee access to the securecloud™, I've lost every fragment of my work from the last few weeks. The black boxes on the live monitor look like empty eye sockets to me. I switch it to standby and move on to the work monitor. I tap on each application individually, each link. Masters didn't forget to sever any connection.

A wave of sickness comes over me. I feel my organs, my stomach, my heart, my intestines shrinking, not working properly anymore.

It's the same feeling I had on the day Andorra disappeared. When she wasn't lying in bed next to me in the morning.

The certainty that she was gone and wouldn't come back.

I remember how my lungs had seemed to shrink. How I could hardly breathe and started gasping for air. How they took me to the infirmary. I can't remember the last sentence I said to her. She nodded off quickly. I kept talking for a little while before realizing she was asleep.

They took her away from me in the middle of the night. And I didn't ask. I knew what had happened.

She didn't say goodbye. Didn't wake me up.

The thought that I slept through it when they led her out of the room—me, the one who always slept so poorly, restlessly. The fact that I was asleep when she gathered her things. That I didn't sense her absence. Until then, I was always absolutely sure that you would feel the loss of the person you loved most. That it would have to tear you apart.

As children, Andorra and I watched a video about a man and a woman who were so closely connected that they could communicate through telepathy. In the video, their connection was tested. They were placed in distant, soundproof rooms. The network was completely blocked. Both were instructed to write down what the other was thinking by hand. They wrote the same thing word for word. Then the conditions were made stricter and the man was asked to paint something. A new microorganism had just been discovered and he was given the first existing picture of it. The woman painted the picture exactly as the man had painted it.

Andorra and I practiced our mind connection the same way. One of us painted a picture and the other one concentrated as hard as she could until the picture appeared in her mind. It worked a few times and we painted the same things. Mostly houses or the sea.

But when she disappeared, I didn't wake up until the alarm clock went off.

It makes me think of Riva when I last saw her: crying on the edge of the sofa, a tiny figure, alone in a big, empty room. The thought of her thin, crumpled body gnaws at me.

I can't leave her sitting there like that.

I want to go to her. To stroke her hair. To tell her every-thing will be fine. To wipe the tears from her face. To ease the pain of having been abandoned. You're not alone, I'd tell her. I'm here. Everything's gonna be okay™.

But I know this impulse is misguided. Unprofessional.

After Andorra's disappearance, I tried to sense her thoughts for a while, to paint pictures she might have just painted or seen. But I couldn't do it and gave up quickly. Another girl moved into my room.

We all accepted the fact that she was gone in the same way you accept a physical flaw that can't be surgically removed. And over time, I remembered Andorra more and more as a temporary phenomenon. A character from a film. She might live on in an imaginary future after the end of the movie, but you won't know anything about her when the credits are over.

I won't let myself get shoved aside so easily. I can't lose Riva. I need to gain access. Get control back. It feels good, knowing what to do. To have clear resolve. To start tak-ing steps towards a solution. To operate like a program right after an update, when all of the software bugs have been fixed.

My stomach calms down as I search for traces of any-thing that the PsySolutions security service may have overlooked. A way back in. All of the computer backup and cache files have been deleted with a data-cleaning service, but the company contacts are still available in the communication channel on my tablet. I take several screenshots and secure them via my private cloud. Never before have I so knowingly committed a criminal act. I should be scared. If I'm discovered, I lose everything. Instead, I feel a sense of satisfaction.

I scan the contact database. I get stuck on one name in

particular. It's like a picture frame that's just the slightest bit crooked and you have to stare at it for a while to figure out what seems off. Zeus Schmidt. There's something about it, a vague memory. It's an ordinary name, nothing conspicuous, but it feels more familiar each time I read it.

My first evening at the retro bar. The missed requests on my tablet when I got home. That name and identification number, now here in front of me on the list. The call, listed under the category *Sexuality*. I remember his voice on the other end of the line. The sound of the headset microphone brushing against his skin. How I told him about my masturbating client. Just like that, without any reason. The man who didn't report me to my employer. Who advised me to delete the call from the log.

His name flickers on the screen like an invitation. He's registered as a freelancer in the data department, so he also works for PsySolutions. He may have processed requests from me in the past, uploaded files for me, entered keywords, created overview graphics. Maybe he recognized my name when I contacted him via the Call-a-Coach™ app. Maybe he watched me on the internal video network in my office afterwards, had his own thoughts on the matter.

Was he a decoy? Could Masters have hired him? Instructed him to somehow lure me into giving the most unprofessional advice possible? Was it a trick to get me to quit my second job and devote all my time to Riva? No. My lack of professionalism wasn't the caller's fault, he didn't do anything to encourage it. I was just so inexplicably worked up, beside myself. No, what made the man stand out was his consideration, his sensitivity. He could have easily initiated complaint proceedings against me. But he helped me instead, tried to end the conversation in such a way that I wouldn't lose face.

I dial his work number without giving it a second thought. He answers after the second ring.

—Good afternoon.

His voice immediately sounds familiar to me.

—Good afternoon.

We're both quiet for a moment. I try to hear the sound of his headset against his skin, but this time he seems to be sitting completely still. I can't hear any sound other than his breath, quiet and even.

—You probably don't remember me, I say. My name is Hitomi Yoshida. You called me a while ago via Call-a-Coach™.

—I remember you.

—I'm sorry for how I behaved back then, I say. It was absolutely outrageous. I've never done anything like that before. One might call it a glitch in the system.

—I like glitches, the man says. They make the system more interesting, don't you think? More open, more flexible. It's like looking into another universe through a random rift that shouldn't exist.

—I wanted to thank you, I say, for reacting so discretely back then. That you didn't report me.

—No problem.

The man's voice sounds calm and pleasantly deep. His breathing is even like a metronome. I imagine his heart rate as a continuous horizontal line that only drops at night.

—I'm sorry to bother you, I say.

—You're not bothering me.

Yesterday, I could have located the man on PsySolutions' internal video system and then watched him talking to me. That is, if he was in the office.

—Are you in the office?

—Home office.

—Me too.

We're both silent again. I listen to his breath. It has an effect on me, like a meditation exercise. I start matching my breathing rhythm to his. I wonder how much time it would take for our hearts to beat at the same rate.

—What can I do for you, Ms. Yoshida?

I hesitate a moment, then I say:

—I also work for PsySolutions. I worked for them. I was fired yesterday.

—I'm sorry to hear that.

It doesn't sound like an empty phrase, I get the feeling that he really is empathetic. That he might even be concerned about me.

—You work for the data department? I ask.

—Yes.

—My account has been blocked. I lost access to the project data and my subject's live video feed.

Suddenly I hear the familiar sound again, the movement of the microphone against his skin. The man is nodding.

—My subject is dear to me, I say. I've invested a lot of time in her. She's already doing much better. I did a good job. It won't take much more to get her back to status quo.

Again I hear the man nodding. His breath is still even.

—I don't want to lose access, I say. I want to finish my job, even if I don't get paid for it. The thought of not knowing what will happen to my subject, how she will progress, is unbearable to me.

—You want me to give you illegal access to confidential company data, the man asks.

I can't tell whether he thinks it's an imposition or a reasonable request. Maybe he's already in the process of informing the security department.

—Is that possible?

—Anything is possible.

—Would you do it?

—We don't know each other, Ms. Yoshida. I would be risking my job for a stranger. Just the fact that you're contacting me through an unencrypted line, on my work number ...

I'm so ashamed that my face turns bright red. I didn't think about the consequences. I didn't even know exactly what I was going to ask him before I called.

—You're right. I don't know where my head is. I didn't think.

—It's okay, I'm using a scrambler. But it's about the principle.

—I understand. I'm sorry that I asked. I don't know what came over me.

—Let the chaos unfold, Ms. Yoshida, the man says. I'll think about it and get back to you

Before I can answer, he hangs up.

I remember why he called the hotline back then. Category: *Sexuality.* A fling with a woman who wasn't sterilized.

Let the chaos unfold, Ms. Yoshida. I suddenly have a strange feeling of a déjà vu. As if this man had said the same sentence to me before in the same way. How does he know how chaotic or orderly my life is? In retrospect, his sentence suddenly sounds stale, as if it came from some sort of daily inspirational content.

32

His message suddenly appears on my tablet. He must have located the device using my data profile. No surprise, I think. He's a data analyst. He's probably put together a complete dossier on me. Probably knows about my unsuccessful date with Royce Hung. About my sleep problems. About every mistake I made working on Riva. Maybe he even watched along with me, saw how Riva and Aston lived, read my logs and notes. Maybe, I think for a moment, he's even watching me now, in this moment, as I discover his message on my tablet. It just showed up there, no notification sound, not in any app. A simple text window:

Are you sure you want a hack? You'd be risking serious criminal charges.

I'm sure, I write in the text window without thinking.

It'll be expensive, Zeus's message appears in the window, *probably more credits than you got for the job in the first place. Is it worth that much to you?*

Yes, I write. *Send me the payment details.*

The payment recipient is listed as the name of a company I've never heard of. The amount exceeds my available credit balance. I choose the installment option on the credit app.

Installments? His message appears above the app window.

Is that okay?

*I'll make an exception. Copy the following login informa-
tion and click on the link.*

The link opens a simple black browser window with a
login form. I hesitate to enter the data. What if Zeus
wants to harm me? Why does a man that I once failed to
counsel seem so trustworthy to me? What if he infects
my device with ransomware or plans to blackmail me
with the hack?

I enter the login data and follow the instructions. The
user interface is identical to my former PsySolutions
account. The video feed from Riva's apartment appears
on the live monitor.

Riva is sitting on the couch as if no time has passed. As
if she had been waiting for me. She sits there like a doll, a
pretty little plastic figurine you can pick up and play
with.

I feel like I did the right thing. I write down the details
of her posture and her eye movements through the room.
I note how she suddenly turns towards the main camera
and stares back at me.

I count the seconds that she keeps staring; it's as if she
can see me behind the camera. At thirty-seven seconds, I
can't stand it any longer. Her eyes are cold and unyield-
ing. Fear begins to spread inside me. Did Zeus tell Riva
about the hack? Did he report me to security services?
Am I being watched?

I suddenly become aware of the full extent of my
actions over the past few days. How could I knowingly
commit these crimes? Why would I violate my professional principles? I see myself sitting in front of my monitors and don't recognize myself. A woman who has sex
with a bartender in a run-down shack in the peripheries.
Who trusts a complete stranger. Who ruins her credit

score to finish an assignment that's not even hers any-more. Who loses the most prestigious job in her career because she hires a person who's a security threat. On a whim.

That's not me.

I'm the girl at the childcare institute who not only fol-lows the rules, but believes in them.

Let the chaos unfold, Ms. Yoshida.

I don't want to let the chaos unfold. I want my life to move forward along the clear paths that I paved with hard work. But I can't undo my actions. Logging out of the hacked account doesn't help. My life has long been infected with malware.

I start shutting down all of the devices anyway. One by one, the monitors, the computer, the router, the servers, the hard drives.

I reach for the tablet, but can't manage to cut this one last connection.

I tap on the parentbot and choose the mother option.

—Hello, my darling, the bot says in its warm, calming voice.

—Mom, I say, I made a mistake. A big one.

Without knowing why, I start to cry. I can't remember the last time I cried that way. Sobbing. Loud, inappropri-ate.

—Everything's gonna be okay™, the voice says. Don't worry, my little one. It'll all be fine.

I nod and sob.

—Just cry it out, she says. Sometimes you just have to cry a little. That's what mothers are for.

I imagine her like the biomother in Zarnee's videos. More voluptuous than city residents, but not fat in an unsightly way. A warm body you can lean into. That wraps around you and protects you from the world.

—Everything's gonna be okay™, the mother says. We'll set it right again. Try to breathe slowly. In. Out. In. Out.

The breathing exercise calms me down immediately.

—Okay, Mom, I say. You're right. Everything will be fine.

I hear her laughing, cooing in a way that makes me think of Royce Hung. Royce in the viewtower™ restaurant. How we laughed together and I felt close to him, even though we'd just met. He probably doesn't even exist, I think. He was probably a field agent like Zarnee, employed by the partnering agency. I've read about such practices. Agencies don't just use bots for online conversations, they also organize staged dates if they think they're in danger of losing a long-term client.

—I'm lonely, I say.

—You have me, the mother answers, I'm always here for you.

When I don't say anything, she starts singing a nursery rhyme, a lullaby I've never heard before. I close my eyes and try a visualization exercise. I imagine the beach and the ocean. Andorra sitting next to me. For a moment, the fantasy works. I can smell the sea, feel the wind on my skin. Then Andorra turns and looks at me, a stern gaze. Penetrating and mean.

—Mom, I say. I made a mistake and now I don't know what to do. I made bad choices, didn't follow the rules.

—Everyone makes mistakes, the motherbot says. Now you just have to set things right again. Tell me what happened and I'll help you.

I try to explain the situation chronologically to her, so I don't miss any details. I start with the interview with Masters, the moment I got the official job offer. How happy it made me. My hopes of career advancement. Social advancement. How I moved into a larger apartment in an exclusive district. How my credit score doubled.

—I am so proud of you, my mother says. You've achieved so much.

When I tell her about how I got fired, she goes quiet. I can feel her disappointment.

—Don't worry, she then says, as if she can read my thoughts. I'm not disappointed. But you're disappointed in yourself. And I want what's best for you.

I nod. My throat feels tight. It's hard for me to find the right words to tell her about the events of the last few days. About Zeus. About his hack. About the lost credits.

—I'll lose my apartment, I say. I'll be deported to the peripheries. I won't be able to come back. All my hard work was for nothing.

—Calm down, my mother says. One step at a time. It's not over yet. We can still find a solution.

—If I could get Riva back to training, back to diving. Make up for it. Then maybe Masters would give me another chance.

—Then do that, my mother says. Do what you think is right, my darling. I believe in you.

33

An invisible man has begun directing Riva's life. I still haven't been able to find out my replacement's name or identification number. The records and tracking software you can buy on the free market are worse than the ones at PsySolutions. Skycam hacks are so expensive that I can't even afford them in installments. I have to resort to cheaper GPS hacks and hope that Riva always has her tablet with her when she leaves the apartment.

Three days ago, Riva was brought to a gym. I tracked her GPS to a fitness club near her apartment. According to her personal data, she had never been there before. The studio's security camera showed her in the company of two men. With one of them standing on either side of her, she signed up for a membership, had a brief introduction, and then trained for forty-three minutes on various machines. She performed each exercise with precision and at an acceptable intensity. The heart rate displayed on the monitor was surprisingly stable, even though she had neglected her body for so long. One of the men gave her a medical exam after the workout. His facial expression showed satisfaction.

Riva's behavior confuses me. She seems balanced, even happy. Zarnee's sudden departure, the knowledge of being observed, she couldn't have just let it all go. When Zarnee made his confession, the way she slowly moved away from him on the couch. How affected she seemed. Slumped down.

I search the log for the recording from that moment, but there's no video footage from that day in the archive. Masters must have removed it to keep it from getting out. From being leaked to the investors. All of the recordings from Zarnee's assignment are missing. The archive footage goes until the day before his arrival and resumes exactly thirty-six hours after Zarnee's departure. It starts up again in the middle of an everyday scene: Riva standing at the kitchen counter, pouring herself a vitamin drink. Her movements have something rehearsed, something artificial. I wonder whether there was a briefing before the recording. A session with Masters. Behavioral advice. Or maybe Masters manipulated the material for the investors.

Shouldn't I be seeing sadness, regression, despair, shock?

How did my replacement manage to achieve such dramatic results within so few days? Is he talking to her personally? Three times, I followed along as Riva was picked up by security and brought to the PsySolutions building. She was registered at the gate and then escorted to the therapy floor. Three times in the same therapy room, number 417. Her facial expression was stoic. It wasn't clear whether she was cooperating.

The publically accessible security camera didn't record the other person, whoever was in the room waiting for her. I reflexively tapped on the encrypted interior view, which I could freely access up until a few days ago. Now I was being shown the standard clauses on the protection of privacy and the punitive fines for hacking. So much is suddenly denied me: I can't see if my replacement is exchanging direct messages with Riva because I no longer have access to the applications on her tablet. I can't see if she's reading her messages or answering them. I've thought several times about asking Zeus to compare my replacement's logs with my own. To check if I missed anything, to see what direction he's going with his investigation. But I still haven't been able to pay off Zeus's hack. My rent for the past month is outstanding. I've already auctioned off most of my valuables. I have to find work again as soon as possible; I need the credits.

I've already increased my availability to twenty-four hours on the Call-a-Coach™ application. But I'm not getting any calls. Maybe I need to reactivate the account. Inform them that I'm available fulltime again. Day and night.

I tap the contact button for technical services. A female voice answers, probably a service bot.

—You're not registered as an employee, she says.

—Since when?

—I'm sorry, we don't need any new employees at the moment, says the voice.

—Can you register me again? I ask. My availability has improved considerably. I can also do day shifts now.

—I'm sorry, we don't need any new employees at the moment, the voice says again.

—I'm already an employee, I say.

—You're not registered as an employee.

—Could you please forward me to a real person?

—I am a real person.

The bots are programmed to ensure that the customer never gets upset in any situation. The communication algorithms contain sets of sentences that are designed to be calming in moments of agitation. Deescalating. Sentences like: I understand how you feel. I want to help. I'm a real person.

—Then a superior? Someone from human resources? I ask.

I look through my archive for the name of a contact person I dealt with in the recruitment process. I'm unsuccessful.

—I'm sorry, we don't need any new staff at the moment, the woman says.

Then she breaks the connection.

Maybe Zeus actually did report me after our call for unprofessional behavior. Then again, maybe Masters was the one who contacted my employer and urged them to remove me from the pool of on-call psychologists.

A notification tone from my tablet informs me that a new video has been published on the Riva-Karnovsky-App™ under the category *Secrets*. Riva is addressing her fans directly for the first time since her resignation.

The video spread to more than three hundred news portals within seconds.

It shows Riva in a changing room. Fans and analysts are already debating whether it's a locker room at the academy or a gym.

Riva looks healthy. She's wearing workout clothes from her biggest sponsor. Her skin is glistening, either from the exercise or from special effects makeup.

—Hey, boys and girls, Riva says. Just a quick shout out: No, I wasn't kidnapped. Haha. I didn't run off with my coach either. Double haha.

At that moment, the camera pans to Dom Wu, who's sitting next to her on the locker-room bench. They've intentionally left some space between them. He smiles and makes a peace sign for the camera. In the live comments, more than fifty people tagged the exact minute and second in the video, pointing out how rare it is to see Dom smiling.

—I'll tell you the truth, Riva says. I just needed a good break. Mindfulness and stuff. But now I'm ready to launch again. Pinky promise.

She leans into the camera and kisses the lens, leaving a lipstick print that distorts the image. Through the blur, you can see her get up from the bench and turn away from the camera.

Something worries me about Riva's behavior. I can't say exactly what, but her sweetly raised voice triggers a kind of inner resistance in me. Is this what rehabilitation looks like? Is that what I've been working towards?

I want to press the replay button, but my right hand has started to tremble. I try to shake it out. It keeps trembling, I can't get it under control.

I look at my hand as it moves uncontrollably. A memory flashes in my mind, a body trembling, shaking, a feeling. My body is shaking, I can't get it under control. More so, I don't want to get it under control. I let it shake, I shake, I surrender to the feeling. My face feels raw. Animal sounds come out of my mouth, roaring and bleating. I look down at myself and have paws instead of hands, fur instead of skin, I feel fangs instead of teeth. I gasp for air, I howl. My body cramps and rears up. I feel a force inside me, an invincible force, I feel every muscle in my body.

And then, suddenly, warmth from behind. Arms wrapping around my body, hands on my face, on my hair, on my neck. I lean into it. It's the most wonderful feeling I've ever experienced. Under the hands, my fur turns to skin. My paws, clawing at the arms around me, are now fingers. My opened snout closes into a smile. My whole body is flooded with warmth.

The memory is so clear.

My skin feels hot with shame. Of course it can't be real. I must have transferred a client's experience to myself, his projections or fears. I must have overidentified with it, a false memory. The images aren't realistic. I would never let myself go like that. But I can't shake the feeling that this false memory evokes in me, the feeling of warmth. I'm filled with a longing to return to that feeling, I want it back with every fiber of my being.

Something is wrong with me. A viral infection. A hormonal disorder. The hand on my skin, I whimper, the body wrapping around me, I want it back.

34

What happened?

The bartender found my number.

You didn't get your job back?

The image of his naked body in the dim light of the bedside lamp.

I saw that you're not listed as a PsySolutions employee anymore. Sorry!

If I don't write him back, he'll assume the number on my profile is wrong.

Come by the bar again.

I wish I could erase moments from my memory the way that Masters erased Zarnee from the observation videos. The encounter with the bartender would be the first thing I'd remove. Getting fired would be the second. Instead, unpleasant memory fragments hover above my thoughts like small lightning storms. The shame that sticks to them is hard to shake off. How I stared at the unevenness of the bare, dark-gray concrete wall in the bartender's apartment. The floor in Masters's Plexiglas office just before fainting. The wire mesh over the intercom at the entrance to the PsySolutions building. A black hair on Andorra's pillow the morning after her disappearance, the depression where her head once was. And the strange foreign memory of the shaking, animal-like body, the embrace.

I can't get rid of it.

The more time I spend doing nothing, the more memory storms there are.

I try to avoid them by concentrating on Riva's analysis. But Riva is hard to find. She's rarely in her apartment anymore.

The facial-recognition search doesn't have any hits for minutes or even hours. I suspect that she's been leaving the building through a secret exit that isn't monitored by security cameras.

Is this Masters's doing? Is it an effort to protect Riva from the cluster of vjs and fans stationed in front of the main building entrance? Or could it be that she's still under Zarnee's influence and has started using illegal methods to protect herself from being tracked?

Because of the legal proceedings, Zarnee's blog keeps getting blocked and then popping up again under different addresses. It has become a refuge for underground political activists. In one of his most recent posts, Zarnee explains how he wears facemasks to disguise himself on excursions into the city. And how he communicates with different black-market tablets that are registered to dead people.

His posts no longer contain idyllic family videos. In a reveal video shortly after his termination, he confessed to his fans that the videos were all staged and that the biofamily was made up entirely of paid actors. He was actually a breeder child who never had parents. The blog served as native advertising for the Family Services™ agency and he has since distanced himself from them. He doesn't want to rent himself out as a family member anymore, he says in the video. Instead, he wants to start a real biofamily. He promises to post real family videos in a few years. Images of a real, natural life. But for that, society will have to go through some drastic changes.

Although most users reacted to Zarnee's revelation with a tidal wave of indignation and character attacks, there are also sympathizers among the commenters. Some news articles have been treating Zarnee as the face of a feared resistance movement. One that could potentially make the extremist positions of the naturals movement more widely accepted. Zarnee claims that his blog's mission has always been political, part of his plan to make society nostalgic and receptive to a more primal way of life. That the success of familymatters.org is a testament to the fact that people feel a deep inner longing to live that way.

His old posts, which used to fill me with a secret and inexplicable pleasure, now fill me with disgust. And bewilderment at the fact that I could fall for an imposter like him. That I put my subject's life in his hands and exposed her to his propaganda, lies, and manipulations.

Riva seems to have resumed many of her past responsibilities. Her apps are constantly updated with new content. In the last few days, she could be seen entering and leaving the academy on several occasions. Gossip and news portals assume that she has resumed training. The posted papavids™ always show Riva accompanied by several security guards. In a few of the fan forums that had previously speculated about Riva's resignation, talk of kidnapping has started popping up again. But other fans always immediately refute the claims with videos and posts from Riva's official apps, pointing out that she obviously seems happy and relaxed as she reports on her life.

35

I've lost Riva. Her facetag hasn't appeared in any facial-recognition searches for fifty-four hours. The apartment and studio are empty. It's as if the earth swallowed her up.

I've had stomach cramps for hours, my whole body is contracting. My fingers can't even keep up with my thoughts on the keyboard, they're like stiff prostheses that don't belong to my body.

According to my activity tracker, I fell asleep at my desk on the day of her disappearance at 1:16 a.m. My body refused to stay awake. I slept for six hours and didn't know where I was when I woke up. My neck hurt so much it was as if I had broken it in my sleep. I could barely hold my head up. When I looked at the monitor, Riva was nowhere to be seen.

Over the last two days, I've tried all of the facial-recognition applications I could afford. None of them delivered results. Then I started clicking my way manually through public security cameras. Riva isn't on any of the streets in her district. She's not in the corridors, elevators, or waiting areas at PsySolutions. Not in the cafes, clubs, bars, or museums that she visited in the past.

I look for clues in the archive feed from the apartment cameras. Riva left the apartment at 3:13 a.m. She was wearing an inconspicuous outfit, no bag. She looked perfectly normal, as if she were just going around the block to get some fresh air because she couldn't sleep. But she never comes back. From the security camera at the corner of her block, you can see her walking away in the dark. After that, she never reappears.

I'm so disappointed in myself that I start trembling. I can't hold back the tears. My body is dried up. I get a glass of water. I take another nootropic pill to avoid falling asleep again.

The feeling of irreversible loss flows through my veins like lead. I know this feeling, it's ingrained in my body.

The empty apartment and the empty room in the institute. The void. Her empty spot next to me at the breakfast table. The others asked about Andorra, I just shrugged. They asked the caregivers. I didn't ask. I heard a caregiver say that Andorra didn't live with us anymore. That she'd been transferred to another institution.

On the previous evening, I had my weekly meeting with the caregiver.

—We caught you, she said.

My body was a pillar of salt. I couldn't respond. She showed me the security video from the elevator. 1:37 a.m.: Me and Andorra wearing short dresses, faces turned away from the camera, so we couldn't be recognized.

—We know that's you, the caregiver said.

—It's disgusting, she said, you're not even sterilized yet. You're a disgrace to your bioparents. They invested all their savings in you. They gave you this exceptional opportunity. I've never seen such ingratitude in my entire life. So much immorality and selfishness. That you would risk destroying your reputation. Destroying your parents' reputations. The institute's reputation. For animal excesses. That's what you did, isn't it? You let us all down for that?

I was shaking so hard that I could barely stand. I shook my head, but I knew it didn't matter. My fate was sealed. My good scores, my future: lost.

—We also know that it wasn't your idea, the caregiver said.

Her voice suddenly sounded different, higher, softer.

—You're a good student, Hitomi. Your adaptation values are high. You're being influenced by an underperformer. You let yourself be tempted.

I looked up to see her facial expression. Her lips hinted at a smile. Then she put her right hand on my shoulder.

—We want to help you. But you also have to help us.

I knew immediately what I had to do. And I didn't hesitate. I had always been good at identifying strategic solutions. At identifying what is expected of me.

—I told her I didn't want to go, I said, but she threatened to sabotage me at the next casting. To make my life hell.

The caregiver's hand was heavy and warm on my shoulder.

—What else?

I listed days and times, left nothing out. When I mentioned Andorra's sleepwalking, the caregiver leaned forward, tilted her head in my direction. She noted down every detail.

—You don't have to feel bad, she said. We want Andorra to get the help she needs.

I nodded. I never stopped nodding.

—We've moved up your appointment for voluntary sterilization, she said, as we parted ways. And you should expect some penalty points. But you'll make it anyway, Hitomi. We believe in your potential.

I can't think clearly. I have to find Riva. I will find Riva. Of course I'll find her. It's only a matter of time. She must be indoors, in a space I can't access anymore. If I had access to the Skycam, I could track where Riva went from her front door, every single step. Wherever she went.

I write Masters. He doesn't reply. I call him. His assistant doesn't want to put me through.

—It's a matter of life and death, I say. You know me. Let me at least explain the situation to him.

The assistant puts me through. Masters's voice is cold and distant.

—Ms. Yoshida. How are you?

—I need access to the Skycam. It's a life and death situation.

—Really?

—Can you help me?

—Life and death? Masters sounds amused.

—Yes.

—Whose life?

—Riva Karnovsky's.

Masters laughs. I hear him shake his head.

—Ms. Yoshida. Listen to me. Riva Karnovsky is no longer your concern. Riva Karnovsky is nobody's concern anymore. She's AWOL, there's nothing we can do about it. Her expulsion order has already been signed. She can't come back. Leave it at that.

—You don't understand. I'm so close.

—You're not close, Ms. Yoshida, Masters says. You've never been close. You failed at your job. Do you know what that failure cost me? I should've fired you back then. Right at the beginning, when you started with childhood. But I'm too soft. I believe in hidden human potential.

—Masters, I say. Please, do me this one favor. I need

the access credentials for the Skycam. For old time's sake.

Masters laughs. Then, abrupt silence. I press my ear against the speaker on my tablet.

There's a soft hum in my apartment. The ventilation fans in the server tower. On the monitor, the split screen displays various security-camera views. Shops, bars, and event spaces where Riva and Zarnee went together. The retro-trash™ bar, where the regulars have already taken their seats. The bartender is wiping down the tables and bar. Subway and skytrain stations. Security cameras from the surrounding streets and squares. I run the facial-recognition software. No matches. Not even partial matches. I look for the latest papavids™ and blog entries with the tags *Riva Karnovsky, Dancer of the Sky, Zarnee, Aston Liebermann*. All of the visual material I find is more than fifty-four hours old.

In the archive, I find a recording from the security camera opposite her apartment building. Riva, Zarnee, and Aston are tagged. It's over a week old. They come out of the building together, engaged in a lively conversation. Riva laughs and touches Aston's hand. They look at each other, a fleeting glance. Then he says goodbye, waves, disappears from the camera's field of vision. Riva and Zarnee stand next to each other for a moment. His shirt collar is folded slightly inwards on the right side of his neck. She tugs it into place.

Maybe she'll come back after all.

I know she's not coming back.

On the monitor, the apartment in the morning light. Empty. Motionless.

The only visible movement is the daylight gliding across the floor on time-lapse mode, the shadows. There are still a few traces of Riva, the unmade bed, a sweater on the living-room table, a blanket hanging off the sofa.

The sofa, where she so often sat with Zarnee, close together like they were a biofamily. Under the right corner of the sofa, I spot the top that Riva had been compulsively spinning at the start of my project. How long it must have been there without anyone noticing.

Suddenly, the images on the split screen drop out simultaneously. All views of the apartment are black, only one exterior view remains. I tap on the black windows to reactivate them. The cameras in the apartment don't seem to work anymore. I try to log in again, but the account no longer exists.

36

I feel a sense of déjà vu, even though I've never set foot in the administration building before. I remember Riva's hesitant steps through the corridors. Her posture, how it revealed her nervousness no matter how hard she tried to hide it.

I walk with determination to avoid making the same mistake. To avoid exposing any weakness. In case Masters is logged in to the security cameras here and watching my movements.

I remember when Riva couldn't find the room and had to turn back. I try to concentrate as I scan the room numbers. 1217A. Even if it doesn't have the same number, the room is identical in terms of furniture and technical equipment.

I sit down in front of the monitor and look directly into the camera.

—Please state your full name and identification number.

—Hitomi Yoshida, MIT 3403 7734 0113.

—Do you fully understand why you're here?

—Yes.

I have an urge to call the motherbot and ask for advice. To tell the mother about the lawsuit that PsySolutions has filed against me. My career is over. My license revoked. Permanent entries in the criminal record, which are displayed at the top of my profile. Removal of company data. Theft of company data. Hacking.

—Would you like to appeal?

The public defender advised me to agree to the expulsion. All legal possibilities have been exhausted. And I have no credits to finance another appeal.

—No, I say.

My voice sounds distant. I have problems recognizing myself in myself. The inner divide that I felt when I was fired has become a sort of permanent state, one part of my consciousness in my body, the other outside it at a distance. Even now, I observe myself from afar, how I'm sitting in front of the camera, keeping my back straight, my shoulders pulled back to signal confidence.

Mom, I want to tell the motherbot, there's nothing I can do. Hugo M. Masters has audio and video recordings from my apartment. From my private devices. From my tablet. The evidence is overwhelming. He also recorded our conversations. Everything I confessed to you. I don't know why I didn't follow the rules. I don't understand it myself, mom.

I won't be able to call the bot. As of this morning, my tablet is also non-operational. The last of my devices that had not yet been turned off. The bill that I had paid the longest until I couldn't get any more credits.

—Then do you agree to relocation on the basis of services not rendered?

—Yes.

Four days ago, in a moment of weakness, I tried to reach my biomother. I called the contact number that was listed in her profile and wrote several messages to the linked M-Message account. When I didn't get an answer, I contacted the company where she's currently registered as a lobbyist, but the secretary refused to put me through.

—Would you like to leave a formal message?

—No.

I can imagine what a disappointment my life must be for them. A wasted investment. An outlier in the official institute statistics, which otherwise say that ninety percent of those leaving city homes make the leap into the top ten percent.

I would also refuse contact in their position. Remove the biochild from my biography so that it doesn't destroy my own career. Another argument for early sterilization. Directly at the age of sexual maturity.

—The relocation measures will be initiated in the next few days, says the gender-neutral voice of the administration computer. We will inform you of the specific conditions electronically. Please sign here.

I use the stylus to put my initials in the blinking field on the form and hold my hand over the fingerprint boxes until a check mark appears.

—We wish you a pleasant day.

I remember how Riva lingered in her seat at this point. How my pulse rose. How I was afraid of Masters's disapproval. One of Riva's many incomprehensible behavior patterns that no longer concern me.

I get up quickly and leave the room. In the hallway, I think about how someone is probably watching me on my way to the exit to make sure I leave the building. The media training at the institute taught me to keep every muscle of my body tensed and my facial expression neutral in these situations. It conveys the image of a competent, highly functioning individual. At least now, on this last official occasion, I would like to act as is expected of me. As I expect of myself. So that if someone should ever go to the trouble of researching my personal data, the last images of me show an upright and self-confident woman. A woman at the height of her career.

Epilogue

The complicated system of walkways and park paths at the ChoiceofPeace™ complex have become as familiar to me as the veins in my forearms. There is no before. The past that brought me here no longer concerns me.

Early in the history of psychology, it was long believed that childhood was decisive in the formation of the human psyche. During my education, I personally doubted modern psychology and its strict exclusion of childhood. My insistence on contemplating the past now seems absurd to me. What determines my life today is not my childhood in the institute, not my youth at business school. Not my work as a business psychologist in the city.

I live the only way worth living: in the present. Our caretakers remind us daily to savor our last weeks, days, hours with all our senses. To make use of the facilities and their numerous wellness offerings. In the seminars, they teach us not to dwell on memories. When clients click through their data archives too often, their caretakers recommend physical fitness, massages, and social events. I understand the need to look back, even if I don't share it myself; it's not out of hope for change, but out of nostalgia or regret. At the end of life, you feel like you have to take stock. A kind of score. I often tell the other clients that the decision for assisted suicide requires us to close the books. Every one of us has considered our credit score, physical state, performance curve, and social status. And we have all come to the conclusion that we can no longer serve society. That the degradation of our bodies, our mental facilities, or our potential for productivity has already reached the point of no return.

Let it all go now, our caretakers say. You've already made the most difficult and responsible decision in your life. Enjoy the fruits of that decision. You don't want to be a burden anymore and we want you to feel light and balanced on your last days. Our sponsors will do everything in their power to make it easier for you to say goodbye.

Because the other co-clients have such a great need to look back, the ChoiceofPeace™ data department now modifies the personal memory apps so that they don't offer any opportunity for remorse. Negative memories are deleted, positive ones added. Depending on the patient's state of mind, they rely entirely on artificial personal profiles, universally acceptable images of a fulfilling life. The artificial profiles achieve the best results on the emotional index.

In my memory app, there are no more court cases, no more forced eviction and relocation. No more arrival in the peripheries, the details of which I have already successfully erased from my mental memory. I am confident that I'll completely forget their existence by my chosen departure date.

I have to struggle with other memories, isolated fragments that are buried deep in my brain in an inexplicable way. Images of Andorra, for example, details of her face repeatedly flash in my mind. The fuzz on her earlobe, sweat on her upper lip. And, even more irrational, the absurd false memory of my own misshapen, disgustingly furry body along with the feeling of warmth that follows. For some reason, I can't erase the sensation of a person's body lying behind me, pressed against me, leaving an imprint on my back. The feeling is deeply embedded in my inner being.

I'm too ashamed to talk to a caregiver about these abnormalities. I have to just hope that they'll fade in the course of our mind-cleansing sessions.

Riva is also still far too clear in my memory and has been even harder to shake off since our chance encounter.

I don't usually leave the facility. I'm repulsed by the peripheries. Just once, shortly after registering at ChoiceofPeace™, I felt drawn outside of its walls. I left the secured area at night, when the temperatures were not as unbearable as during the day and the crowds had hopefully already returned to their hovels. A strange curiosity came over me, an inner restlessness that I wanted to satisfy before living out my final days.

I walked the streets without a specific destination. The rectangular apartment blocks reminded me of the bartender's apartment, although his home had seemed almost luxurious compared to the buildings here. Even in the peripheries there seem to be certain hierarchies, better and worse districts. Internal rules that are not easily recognized by outsiders.

I tried to walk along roads where there were very few other people. Whenever anyone walked past me, I kept my head down so that no one would try to approach me. I had been walking for about half an hour when I saw Riva.

It was a complete surprise; I wasn't prepared for it. She came towards me, our paths crossed right in the beam of light beneath a street lamp. I recognized her immediately, even though her face and body had changed. She had gotten rounder. Her figure was voluptuous, wrapped in a short summer dress that reminded me of the one she had worn on the first day of video analysis. Her face looked younger. When I recognized her, her name instinctively came across my lips.

—Riva, I shouted, without thinking about it. She stopped and looked at me.

—Do we know each other? she asked.

I hesitated for a moment because I didn't know what she meant.

I wanted to say: Don't you remember me?

Even after all these months, she still seemed so familiar to me. I had the urge to touch her. During the analysis, I often felt like Riva knew about my existence, knew that I was behind the camera. Her movements, her few words seemed directly addressed to me, an invitation to decipher her soul. But now I was looking into the face of a stranger. Friendly, but distant.

I considered telling her about my assignment. Asking her where she lived now. Why she had left her apartment so suddenly. I wanted to ask her about Aston and Zarnee.

I know you, I wanted to say, I know you well. I almost managed to get you to dive again. Your life was in my hands.

—I was a fan, I said instead. I went to one of your performances when I was a kid. Too bad you stopped so early.

Riva shrugged.

—It was time, she said.

I nodded, I wanted to say something else, keep her with me for a moment. Talk to her for a bit. But she had already started walking away.

—Nice to meet you, I said.

She politely shook my outstretched hand. I felt the

rough surface of her skin between my fingers. She works with her hands, I thought, somewhere in the peripheries.

I watched her disappear into the twilight. She had a lightness to her steps that I'd never seen from her before. Even after the rest of her had disappeared, her arms and legs fading into the distance, her brightly colored dress was still visible for a while.

I considered following her. To see where she lived. If the others were there, too. I took a few steps in her direction, but then I stopped myself. I thought about what my caretakers had advised me to do. To concentrate on the present. Riva was no longer a part of my life.

Still, as I made my way back to the ChoiceofPeace™ grounds, I felt a strange emptiness. It was as if an organ had been removed from my body. I had never known a person more intimately than Riva, not even Andorra. And yet there was no connection between us.

My body tensed up. I had to sit down on the dusty street and lean against a wall. I sat like that for a while, hunched in the dark. I tried to fill the emptiness inside me with breath. I did various breathing exercises, but nothing helped. Then I tried a visualization.

In one of the seminars where they teach us to overcome the fear of death, we learned a visualization exercise. We were advised to do it at the moment of the procedure. We practice it over and over again in preparation. We are instructed to visualize a high-rise diver. The dive.

Imagine your body in eternity, the caregiver tells us. Look for an image that makes you feel like death doesn't exist, only life.

I closed my eyes and tried to imagine Riva as a young high-rise diver. Standing at the edge of the dive platform against the light. Her symmetrical silhouette, her power.

When I couldn't picture it, I tried to imagine rising up out of the scene, up above the city. Soaring like a bird. The city getting smaller and smaller until it finally merged into a uniform surface, a glittering sea far beneath me. I closed my eyes, concentrated all of my thoughts on it.

But no picture would appear.

Thank you

Frank: for, you know, everything.

Nazanine: without you I would not have dared to be a writer.

My bioparents Ingeborg and Franzeff: for a genetic literary disposition, basic psychotherapeutic upbringing, and the credit points.

Karsten: for the great, in no way Lish-like editing.

Clemens: for your books and your astronaut support.

Silvio: for your faith in the text.

Martina and Lulu: for your eyes on the text and crisis intervention.

Florian: for Thomas and Thomas: for Karsten.

My literary classmates and teachers for your companionship, especially Ruth, Verena, Regina, Marina, Sara, Maria, and Baba for your help with this novel.

And to everyone else who ever had anything to do with this text.

SHARMILA COHEN is an award-winning writer and German-to-English translator who has translated the works of several leading German-language authors. Her work has been featured in publications such as *BOMB* and *Harpers*, and her projects span from poetry and literary fiction to crime and children's stories. Originally from New York, Cohen came to Berlin in 2011 as a Fulbright Scholar to complete an experimental translation project with local poets. She now divides her time between both cities.

On the Design

As book design is an integral part of the reading experience, we would like to acknowledge the work of those who shaped the form in which the story is housed.

Tessa van der Waals (Netherlands) is responsible for the cover design, cover typography, and art direction of all World Editions books. She works in the internationally renowned tradition of Dutch Design. Her bright and powerful visual aesthetic maintains a harmony between image and typography and captures the unique atmosphere of each book. She works closely with internationally celebrated photographers, artists, and letter designers. Her work has frequently been awarded prizes for Best Dutch Book Design.

The color combination of silver, black, and yellow has been chosen for its futuristic techno effect. The font is called "Empire," and was originally designed by Morris Fuller Benton in 1937. These titling capitals became the headline style for *Vogue* magazine, and later on for *Publish* magazine in a restyled and expanded version by David Berlow. The extremely high and narrow letters create a feeling of height and depth, suggesting skyscrapers for the diver to jump from. The drawing of the diver was created by Annemarie van Haeringen, an internationally renowned Dutch illustrator.

The cover has been edited by lithographer Bert van der Horst of BFC Graphics (Netherlands).

Suzan Beijer (Netherlands) is responsible for the typography and careful interior book design of all World Editions titles.

The text on the inside covers and the press quotes are set in Circular, designed by Laurenz Brunner (Switzerland) and published by Swiss type foundry Lineto.

All World Editions books are set in the typeface Dolly, specifically designed for book typography. Dolly creates a warm page image perfect for an enjoyable reading experience. This typeface is designed by Underware, a European collective formed by Bas Jacobs (Netherlands), Akiem Helmling (Germany), and Sami Kortemäki (Finland). Underware are also the creators of the World Editions logo, which meets the design requirement that "a strong shape can always be drawn with a toe in the sand."